Praise for Patricia A. McKillip's *Moon-Flash*

"Rare ... beautiful ... a lovely work."

— *Science Fiction Review*

"Absorbing ... lyrical.... The reader is drawn into Kyreol's world, exploring it with her and sharing the insights that come to her."

— *Fantasy Review*

"A fully successful move into new territory ... the eloquence will satisfy all McKillip fans."

— *Locus*

"Marvelously imaginative ... a great deal of action and adventure ... highly recommended."

— *Rochester Post-Bulletin*

"Fascinating ... striking ... vividly detailed."

— *Desert News*

"A powerhouse of ideas.... The reader travels ... through the ages of humankind."

— *English Journal*

"A tale of discovery ... interesting ... romantic.... This book is good fun to read."

— *Science Fiction and Fantasy Forum*

Berkley books by Patricia A. McKillip

THE FORGOTTEN BEASTS OF ELD
THE MOON AND THE FACE
MOON-FLASH
STEPPING FROM THE SHADOWS

PATRICIA A. McKILLIP

The Moon
and the
Face

BERKLEY BOOKS, NEW YORK

THE MOON AND THE FACE

A Berkley Book / published by arrangement with
Atheneum Publishers

PRINTING HISTORY
Argo Book edition published 1985
Berkley edition / October 1986

ISBN: 0-425-09206-2

A BERKLEY BOOK ® TM 757,375
Berkley Books are published by The Berkley Publishing Group,
200 Madison Avenue, New York, NY 10016.
The name "BERKLEY" and the stylized "B" with design
are trademarks belonging to Berkley Publishing Corporation.

PRINTED IN THE UNITED STATES OF AMERICA

The Moon and the Face

1

TERJE SAT on the bank of the River, gazing at the reeds and yellow flowers that filled the shallows. He was just south of Arin Thrase's museum; he had walked there in three days from Domecity. He was waiting for Kyreol.

A hawk circled above his head, gold as the desert the river divided. A bullfrog droned somewhere among the reeds. The sun had just risen; the slow green water misted toward the light. Terje sat very quietly, letting thoughts slide through his head like cloud reflections sliding across the water. He was dressed in skins and a feather vest. A feather band around his thigh held his knife; a pocket inside one soft boot held his com-crystal. He had let his hair grow shaggy for a few weeks. Leaning over the water, that dawn, he had painted his face. The face gazing back at him belonged to two people: Terje of the Dome and a young hunter of the Riverworld, tall and muscular, his fair skin and hair burned gold with sun-

3

light, his face calm, motionless from long hours of listening for the stir of animals in the brush.

He saw silver flash in the water and turned his head. The little pickup craft Kyreol flew was virtually soundless, for the stations they flew to were often deep in protected territory. It was landing now, not so silently, kicking up dust from the hot, arid ground. Terje, who had spent the past days in solitude beside the peaceful River, blinked at the craft as if it had fallen off a star. Then he gathered his few belongings and rose.

Kyreol opened one door of the pickup craft; Regny Orcrow, also dressed in feathers, opened the other. Terje stared at him, surprised; he kissed Kyreol, leaving a smudge of paint on her face, before he spoke.

"What are you doing here?" he asked Regny. "You said this time I was going to the Riverworld alone."

"I know," Regny said.

"It's just the early autumn ritual."

"I know," Regny said again. "I know what I said." He leaned against the pickup craft, his vest of dappled gold and dark feathers looking a little bedraggled. A crow feather drifted to the ground. Kyreol grinned.

"You're moulting."

Regny sighed. "I was supposed to have a new vest made before I went back up."

Terje slid his fingers through his hair. "What is it? Is something wrong?"

"It's my mother," Kyreol said. "She changed her mind."

Regny shrugged. "I don't know. You've been training for four years; you've been to the Riverworld with me or another agent over a dozen times. I thought you were more than ready to observe by yourself, since you know the Riverworld so well. Nara said she thought so, too. But this morning she changed her mind. She told me to come with you. She's the boss."

"But why?" Terje said again, patiently, looking at Kyreol. She shook her head a little, her dark face perplexed.

"We didn't have much time to talk. She just—I don't know. Maybe she had a dream about you that worried her, so she decided to send Regny."

"What could happen to me in the Riverworld?"

"Well, I don't know, Terje. You could fall out of a tree; you could eat a bad musk-berry; you could shoot yourself by accident—"

"With an arrow?" He was smiling, remembering then the long hours they had spent together before he had gone upriver. The sun caught in her eyes; she laughed, suddenly very close to him, though he couldn't remember which of them had moved. He touched her cheek, thinking, at its sunlight darkness, of the black, immense slab of rock that had shrugged its way out of the earth to become, eons later, the northern boundary of the Riverworld. The child-woman Kyreol, betrothed and swarming like a beehive with questions, had drawn him past the edge of the ancient Riverworld into the future. But she wasn't a child now. She was Kyreol of the Dome, slender

5

and tall in a silver flightsuit, with the reflection of the Face in her skin and the shadow of its secrets in her eyes.

Their memories drew them closer; their mouths touched. Regny cleared his throat. "Come on. You'll see each other again in six weeks. We have to fly halfway up this river by noon. You want me to pilot, Kyreol?"

She shook her head. "I want to. I'm getting better at it."

"What's that supposed to mean?"

"Well, I get distracted," she explained, letting Terje in first. "There are so many things I want to look at, I just forget where I'm going."

"Oh, fine," Regny grumbled. "Not only am I back to work when I'm supposed to be on vacation, but I'm in the hands of an absentminded pilot." He climbed in, shedding a couple more feathers.

Terje said suddenly, "She could have sent someone else. Another agent instead of you."

"She wanted me to come with you. That's all I know. I don't know why. She just told me to go . . ." He was silent, his black face indrawn, unblinking: the face of the hunter, silent and full of mysteries, that had lured Kyreol years before beyond her world. When the engines had quieted and the small craft had begun its meandering course around the protected areas, he added, "I've known Nara about as long as I've known the Riverworld. That's long enough to know that sometimes asking questions isn't the best way to get an answer. Sometimes you just wait."

"Was she upset about something?"

"What I'm trying to say," Regny said patiently, "is that she didn't know why either."

"That doesn't make sense. She wouldn't send you to the Riverworld for six weeks without a good reason."

"She had a good reason."

"Well, what was it?"

"She wasn't sure." He caught Terje's eye and smiled. "Don't worry. Kyreol must be right. Nara probably just had a dream, and maybe she couldn't remember what it was, but it had something to do with you, so she thought she'd better send me—"

"Why didn't she just tell me not to go?" Terje asked bewilderedly. "If it was that important?"

"Oh, Terje," Kyreol said. "You're not listening."

"I am listening. And I'm making more sense than anyone else."

"You're only listening with your ears. She just knew she should send Regny. That's all. So she did. Later, you'll know why."

"That doesn't make me feel very secure."

"Terje, if you were going to be in danger, she wouldn't have let you go. Besides, nothing ever happens in the Riverworld."

"That doesn't make—" He stopped, sighing. Regny reached back, gripped his shoulder lightly.

"Don't worry about it. You can go alone next time. The only thing I'm worrying about is whether or not this vest will hang together for six weeks. I hate sewing feathers."

The land flowed beneath them like a gold sea, barren and wrinkled, scarred with heat, sculpted by wind. Only the River, burrowing out of the northern forests, gave it a fiercely glittering thread of color. Near noon, the dust began to melt into green. The land reared upward, jaggedly, on both sides of the River. The tangled brush and stunted trees flowed into vast, deep forest, stretching northward as far as the eye could see. A tree flashed beneath them, another—

"Bring it up," Regny murmured, and Kyreol eased the small craft upward.

She said apologetically, "My eyes keep wanting to watch things, and then my hands follow my eyes . . ." Her voice sank to an awed whisper. "Look at that. I never knew it was so beautiful."

Ahead, the Face rose out of the forest, the great black cliff half-hidden beneath the rainbow-filled mist of its Falls. A deep lake set like a jewel in solid stone was the birthplace of the Falls. The river fed the lake, coming southward from yet another blue-black forest; far, far ahead, there was another thumb-print of black rising above the trees, another face of stone crowned with another lake . . .

"It's like steps down the world," Kyreol breathed. "A giant's threshold."

"You're over protected area," Regny said quickly. "You overshot the landing point."

"Where?" She angled away from the forest just as her receiver crackled.

"North Outstation Five to PC103D. What course are you trying to follow?"

"It's me, Kyreol. I'm coming down."

"Kyreol!" exclaimed the voice. "Welcome back. Try not to land on my roof."

"There," Terje said, looking down at a bald spot near the western edge of the forest, just at the line where the river mists yielded to the sun and the desert reclaimed the land once more. Kyreol was silent, concentrating. They flew on a level with the treetops. Then they were down, bumping across the ground, the ancient trees towering over them.

They got out tiredly, stretching. The birds were settling back into the trees, little flashes of lemon, chartreuse, scarlet, scolding fiercely. Then they subsided, and there was just the wind, with its invisible weave of messages Terje was learning to separate: animal smells, the smell of honey, the smell of rain.

He saw Kyreol, her arms folded as she lounged against the pickup craft, watching him wistfully. He had vanished for a moment, behind his hunter's face. He was doing something she would never permit herself to do: returning to the Riverworld, disappearing back into a memory, a dream.

He went to her, put his arms around her. "I'll miss you," he said softly. "It's always strange, being there without you. It's my home, the place where I was born, but I can't speak to anyone, I can't let myself be seen, I'm invisible . . . I visit all the places you and I explored when we were little, but you're not there anymore."

"I'm glad Regny's with you. Six weeks is a long time to be invisible."

"It will go fast."

"I'll miss you." She sighed. "I won't have anything to do but work. Except . . . There's something I haven't told you. I didn't want to tell you, because I didn't want you to think about it while you were here. But maybe I should, because if you have any peculiar dreams with me in them, dreams that don't make sense—"

"Kyreol—"

"Don't worry about them; I'll be back before you get back and you won't even know I've been gone—"

"What—"

"I'm just going to Xtal."

"Xtal," he said blankly, his hands slack on her shoulders. Then he shouted, "Kyreol, that's another planet!"

The birds started squawking again. Regny, who was unloading their gear, turned to stare at Terje.

"What's wrong?"

"She's going to another planet!"

"Just Xtal," Regny said soothingly. "That's not far."

"It's—it's—" He gestured wordlessly, his hands arcing above his head. Kyreol nodded, her brows crinkled.

"Well, Terje," she said reasonably. "This is what the Agency has been training me for. To study small cultures like the Riverworld, only on other planets. How can I study them if I never see them?"

"Why do you have to see them now?" he demanded unreasonably. "Now, while I'm here in the wilderness, instead of at the Dome, where I'll know if you've landed safely, if you—Kyreol, it's not like a river journey. If you fall out, there's nothing to swim in, there's no shore to swim to—"

"It's a little hard to fall out of a spaceship."

"You know what I mean."

"I know, but there's nothing to worry about. Joss Tappan's been in space a hundred times; he'll be with me. I'll only be there three weeks; I'll be back before you are. If you'd like, I'll send a message to the Outstation when I do get back. And I'll pick up you and Regny when you're ready to come back. I promise: Nothing will happen to me."

"Then why didn't you tell me this before?"

She was silent. She put her arms around him suddenly, her cheek against his cheek. "Because I'm scared," she said softly, and felt his arms circle her. "It's not the dark I see in dreams that I'm going into. It's a night of nothing. It's just a means of getting from point to point, but it's so vast, and the planet I'm going to is so different, that how will I remember who Kyreol is? I don't know if you can take your past from planet to planet." She stopped, laughing a little. "I'm not saying it right. It's just— It will be different. I hope I won't be different, with my mind full of alien things."

He drew back from her slightly, looked at her, as if he were almost hearing something she wasn't saying. "You're the same Kyreol I grew up with in the Riverworld. Living in the Dome changed some things about you, but not—not the things I love."

"I know." Her eyes were hidden against him; her voice came muffled by his collarbone. "One thing changed. I could never go back to the Riverworld."

He opened his mouth, closed it. She lifted her head quickly, then, smiling. "It will be all right. In six weeks, I'll come and get you. I'll tell you stories about the Burrowers of Xtal. They live in caves because they

11

can't endure light; their eyes are huge, like owls' eyes, only colorless, and they paint the future on their walls."

He didn't smile. He brushed her cheek gently with his fingers. "Did you have a dream?" he asked. The forest was very still; Regny, who was filling the inner pockets of his boots with obscure, miniscule equipment, lifted his head to listen.

"No. Maybe that's what's bothering me. I try to see ahead, awake or asleep, and all I can see is—" She gave a little, helpless shrug. "Nothing."

"Kyreol. You're scaring me."

"Oh—" She smiled again and kissed him swiftly. "I'll see you again. That's the only thing I do know."

HE THOUGHT about that, much later, as he lit a fire from a piece of flint, deep within the Riverworld. Regny had gone for water. They had hiked all afternoon; by evening they were close to the River, but down from the Face, away from the small stone houses along the banks. The flint sparked; a dry leaf flamed. He dropped it into a nest of dry twigs, then added wood slowly, nursing the fire patiently, tuned once again to the slow, painstaking habits of the Riverworld. The warmth touched his face. He sat back, thinking of Kyreol.

Regny stepped into the circle of his fire so quietly he startled, then looked up as Regny slipped the water-skin straps off his shoulders and sat down.

"Dinner ready?"

Terje handed him some dried meat. Regny contemplated it. "For this I traveled half a continent." He chewed a few moments, then said: "Seems quiet. I watched the moon rise above the Face. The whole river turned silk white. It made me remember why I came back. Why I keep coming back . . ."

Terje lifted his face toward the stars, thick as pebbles in the bed of a deep black river. "Did you see any of the hunters?"

"No." He stopped, listening to a faint crackling in the dark. It subsided after a moment. "The only thing I saw that moved was a fire."

"This fire?"

"No. It was upriver; it moved across the water. Somebody in a boat carrying a torch."

"That's odd. Usually, if it's night, they just go to sleep." He added with his mouth full, "Anyway, on a night like this, who needs a torch?"

They were silent. Twigs in the fire curled and snapped; sap keened. Something tiny scurried away from them. A bird cried once. Terje's eyes rose from the fire; he questioned Regny puzzledly, wordlessly. Torchlight under a full moon? Fire on the water?

"Lamplight, maybe, on a boat. But uncovered fire —that's only for ritual. And it's the wrong time of the year for that one."

"All right," Regny said softly, and stood up. "Let's take a walk and find out."

2

THE DOME seemed almost unbearably bright and noisy to Kyreol when she returned: too full of people threading purposeful paths through intricate and bewildering machinery. The dock crew complimented her on her first flight alone. She responded tiredly, wishing there was something—a tree with a bird in it, a pool full of sunlight—she could rest her eyes on. The colors and smells of the Riverworld still lingered on the edge of her mind. She had already begun to miss Terje.

She left the dock, took a central elevator up to the top of the Dome. The shields that protected the inner Dome from blazing light during the day were open to reveal the silver scythe of the moon and stars so thick they blurred together into a twinkling mist.

She stopped beside the roof-garden, gazing up at the stars. The sheer numbers of them made her dizzy. She could scarcely find the pinprick of white fire to which she would be flying in two days. She felt a sudden, dismaying depression as she studied the night.

All her excitement over the new journey, the unexplored place, had vanished.

I'm just tired, she thought. *But it's so far away . . . So far from everything I know . . . I wish . . .* But she didn't know what she wished. She saw her mother, then, coming out of one of the circle of doors around the roof, and she smiled, feeling less lonely.

Nara hugged her, as if she had been gone a month rather than a day. They were very much alike. Looking at her, Kyreol thought, was like looking at a reflection in still water. Only their voices were different. Nara's was gentle, husky; she treated words carefully. Kyreol's voice, bright, impulsive, usually showered words in the air like puffball seeds. But she was feeling quiet, then; she just said, "Everything went fine. I flew all the way, both ways."

"That's wonderful," Nara said. "But you look very tired. Come and eat supper."

"Terje was surprised to see Regny."

"I thought he might be."

Kyreol sighed. "I miss Terje."

"In two days," Nara said, "you'll be too busy to even think about him." She opened the door to their small, elegant quarters. Music was playing; her scarlet and gold birds were singing to it. A rich, spicy smell from the kitchen hung in the air. Kyreol sniffed and some of her tiredness eased away.

"You cooked for me!" In four years she had gotten used to food dried and frozen and summoned up out of a wall dispenser.

"You and Joss Tappan. He's joining us in a few moments."

"Oh."

Nara smiled. "Kyreol, he wants to talk to you a little more about your journey to Xtal. Go take a shower and change out of your flightsuit. You'll feel more like thinking then."

Which, Kyreol discovered as she pulled a bright, loose robe over her head and combed out her wet hair, was true.

Joss Tappan was sitting among Nara's cushions when Kyreol came back out. She greeted him shyly, for though she liked him, she was awed by him. He was the Head of the Interplanetary Cultural Agency; his agency trained observers for other planets the way Nara's trained them for the world below. He was a tall, fair-haired man with startling eyes in a deeply tanned face. His eyes were so clear they seemed almost colorless, like water. They reminded Kyreol of the eyes of the Burrowers of Xtal: luminous and full of secret visions.

But he wasn't a secretive man. He was open, friendly, and full of boundless curiosity about alien cultures. From him and his agents, Kyreol was learning three major off-world languages; she was studying the cultural histories of Xtal and Omolos, its inhabited moon; her head was full of dates, land-forms, strange rituals, and even stranger descriptions of aliens, the way they evolved into such unfamiliar shapes and why.

He gestured to the cushions beside him, and she sat in a billow of fiery cloth. Nara had set their meal on a low table, so they could eat comfortably as they talked.

"Are you looking forward to the journey, Kyreol?" Joss asked, and at the warm, expectant smile in his eyes, she began to feel once again the stirrings of excitement. Nara came in with hot bread and beer for Joss. She poured tea for herself and Kyreol, then sat down with them.

"I'm excited," Kyreol said, tearing a chunk of bread. "I'm also scared to death."

"That's natural," Joss said. "Some people love space flight. Others get space-sick; they can't stand being away from Thanos, or they find themselves terrified of the vastness of space. We'll see what kind of traveler you are. I heard you had a perfect flight to Outstation Five. That's a good sign."

"Well. Not quite perfect. I was so busy looking at where the River came from, I forgot where I was going."

"I don't blame you. It is beautiful up there."

"Is Xtal beautiful?"

"Most of it looks like a dust bowl and smells like bad eggs," Joss said cheerfully. "Some of the canyons of colored sand, the wastelands of obsidian, the lichen forests growing out of volcanic ash are to me amazingly beautiful. But then," he added, smiling at her expression, "I can be pleased by almost anything. Except the smell of sulphur. We wear small filters, by the way, which purify the air of irritants." He filled his plate with stew, then added, "That's one way we learned that the Burrowers possess the ability of foresight. I was the first agent to visit them. When I entered their caves, the first thing I saw was a tall, fair-haired human with a nose filter on, painted on the cave wall. They couldn't have seen me coming; they aren't able to look directly into light."

Kyreol thought of the photograph she had seen of a pair of enormous, silvery eyes belonging to a vague, shadowy shape, on the verge of ducking back into darkness.

"It's their wall paintings I want you to study," Joss said. "They're like nothing you will ever have seen. Great clouds of color, abstract designs. Yet even colors have significance and, sometimes, a reference to future events that might disturb them—such as volcanic activity or strangers coming."

"Do they like strangers?"

"They seem to. There are never more than two or three of us at one time, and we space our visits. They've learned our names; sometimes they give us small gifts. Generally, they go about their daily business undisturbed by us."

Kyreol chewed a bite of stew. Visions of the journey through the dark of space, her world growing tinier and tinier until it merged into the glittering mist of stars, of her first, irrevocable step onto an alien world, made the bite stick in her throat. Her hands felt cold. She frowned, trying to mask her fear from Joss. If she was to be an interplanetary agent, this would be only the first of many journeys.

But he saw her fear, and asked anxiously, "Are we asking too much of you, Kyreol of the Riverworld? You have many gifts I want to test in other cultures. But only if you want that. You don't have to go to Xtal. You never have to leave Thanos, if you choose not to."

But that made her feel restless, as though there was not room enough on one world for her. She laughed at herself, then said slowly, "I want to go to Xtal. As long as there's a place with a name that I haven't been to, I'll be curious about it. It scares me to think of stepping off this world. What if I can't get back on? But I still want to go. I want to see the cave paintings. I want to see how the Burrowers draw their tomorrows."

They talked of practical matters then: of what she should pack, how long the flight would take, what time they would leave. When Joss Tappen left, it was very late. The Dome was hushed. It seemed at that moment to Kyreol a tiny planet in itself, the people within it different from those who lived on the ancient, living earth below. *If I step even farther*, she thought, *will I change even more? Will Terje know me when I get back?* The thought made her throat burn. *I should have gone with Terje.* She turned restlessly, pacing a little, not realizing she had spoken the words aloud. She found Nara watching her, seated on the cushions, her eyes grave, her dark face very still.

"You sense it, too," she said abruptly, and Kyreol, startled, stopped mid-pace. Relief ran through her, that her feelings had a name, even though the name was trouble.

"I'm uneasy," she said. "I don't know why. What is it?"

"I don't know either," Nara said helplessly. "I'm not a Healer, or a Healer's daughter. Foresight is not my gift. I just feel—" She stood up and went to

Kyreol, took Kyreol's hands between her own, smiling, though the worry still filled her eyes. "I just keep wanting to protect you all from something—you, Terje, Regny, Joss—but I have no idea what it is. And there's nothing I can do. Except wait until you are safely beside me again." She touched Kyreol's cheek, her smile deepening, and Kyreol felt soothed. "We've been on long journeys, you and I. Stepping out of the known world has its price. But the rewards are incalculable."

FOUR DAYS LATER, Kyreol watched an enormous freighter, all dark planes and cities of winking lights, crawling through the void slowly as a caterpiller compared to their swift hawk-flight. They caught up with it, passed over it; it blurred into shapeless streaks of light. It was, she thought, the most exciting thing that had happened in hours.

As they left Thanos she had watched her world and her moon grow small enough to hold in her arms—smoothly, brightly beautiful, one gold-blue, one ice-white, like bubbles, adrift in a vast dark. The sun burned like a torch in the night, casting shadows that spanned thousands of miles. The distance between one bubble of fire or rock or water and another seemed overwhelming. That the distance had been breached, the empty silence, so different from the private silence of dreams, had been broken at all was astonishing.

"Five hundred years ago," Joss Tappan had told her, "it would have taken us months to get to Xtal.

Now the Dome has a routine flight across the system; the entire flight takes less than two weeks. We learned a great deal when we began comparing our technology with that of alien cultures."

The River here was black, deep; the shores were of white fire, too far even to consider. The stepping stones were isolated worlds. Even at the speed with which their small ship streaked through space, there were hours on end when Kyreol saw little besides swarms of dust and ice particles gleaming momentarily, like fireflies, in its light. Even that fascinated her: the desert of time and distance between one handful of dust and the next.

I love it, she thought, all her worries dissipated. She felt insignificant as a fly, yet proud that she was part of the thinking beings who had told themselves a story of traveling through space, and then found the way to make the story true. The path through the dark was old and familiar; countless people had gone ahead of her to make it safe. Remembering them, she forgot her fear, and all her odd sense that despite the serenity of the flight, there might indeed be something to fear.

It was while they were passing the planet between Thanos and Xtal—the giant water bubble called Niade with its eighteen moons—that trouble came out of nowhere. It was as if a hand out of the dark struck them with a terrifying force, sent them spinning toward those moons, toward that looming water, toward the bottomless deep beyond.

3

THE HUNTERS stood still within the shadows flowing from the moonlit trees. Behind them, the water pouring down the Face thundered its constant, powerful chant, then gradually grew deep, slow, near the place where the hunters hid. They were watching a cluster of small, bobbing boats anchored in the River, illumined by moonlight and by the fire of torches held aloft. The reflections of fire streaked across the dark water toward the Healer's house.

A chant began, low, indistinct. Terje's hair twitched slightly in a puzzled shake. "What is it?" he whispered. His words had little more sound than a nightmoth's wings under the chanting and the distant roar of the Falls. Regny drew breath softly, easing his stance one muscle at a time.

"I've never seen anything like it . . . I don't recognize the chant."

"It's something to do with the River. They keep asking it something—" He made another abrupt, tiny movement. "We have to get closer." Regny's hand closed above his elbow, and he stilled.

There was a faint crackling of leaves, no more sound than a beetle might make, foraging. Terje looked out of the corner of his eyes. A hunter passed them, not stalking, but walking in his normal way, his bare feet automatically adjusting his weight to pass noiselessly across whatever twig or dry leaf happened to be underfoot. They watched him move toward the Healer's house and stop, merge into the silence of the trees around him.

Terje whispered, "He's watching, too."

"There will be others. Stay still."

"But what is it?"

"You're asking me? You were born here."

"You should know," Terje said reasonably. They listened. A few more boats, poled upriver, were joining the cluster. The chant seemed no more than a murmur, rising and falling rhythmically, like breathing. Another hunter appeared briefly in the moonlight, slipped into the shadows around the Healer's house. Something in their secrecy made Terje think not of rituals but of wild things drawn toward warmth, or toward something unfamiliar. Or toward—

"You should know," he said again. The pitch of his voice made one hunter turn his head, scan the night.

Regny had gathered breath, but he held it until the hunter turned away again. Then he breathed, "Calm down. Or else go wait downriver."

"I'm sorry."

"You should be."

"Regny, what is it? The whole Riverworld is watching the Healer's house. It's night, they're chanting to the River, there's no feasting, no Moon-Flash, so it can't be a betrothal; they seem to be waiting—they seem . . ." His voice faded uncertainly. Regny answered after a moment, his face holding no more expression than a stone.

"I've never seen it before. But the darkness, the fire, the chant to the River—they're reminiscent of the mid-year ritual."

Terje glanced at him quickly, involuntarily. "The naming of the dead. But this isn't a death ritual. The Healer gives the dead back to the River."

"I know."

"Maybe he's doing some kind of special Healing. That must be it." He brooded, his eyes on the stone house, its round windows rippling with fire. "Regny, we have to get closer."

"The house is surrounded by hunters. You'd be recognized."

"There are other fair-skinned hunters. I wouldn't be that conspicuous."

"You would be with your head through the window."

Terje was silent, frowning. Another hunter passed them, an older man, with grizzled hair and black feather armbands. Seeing two men dimly in the moonlight, he gave them a hunter's greeting, showing his palm with his sign on it, then went on, silent as an owl in the night. Regny loosed his breath slowly.

"It's getting crowded around here. We should separate."

"Listen."

The chant had stopped. A night breeze stirred through the trees, left a moonlit hush in its wake. The moon had grown distant, shriveled. A petal of fire dropped from one boat into the water. Then another. The boats, their bows lamplit, were turning downriver. The hunters watched silently for a long time until the last golden star of light had glimmered away into the darkness. Then Terje whispered, "Now. Now we can see."

"I'll go."

"I'm coming."

"No."

Terje opened his mouth, closed it. He said patiently, "If you weren't with me, that's the decision I would make."

Regny's impassive face relaxed a little. "I know. You should be here alone, and I shouldn't be telling you what to do. But you're not, and I am. The Healer is an extraordinary man. You know that. One glimpse of your face and he'd be asking so many questions we'd both be out of a job. Bear with me. We're both here, and it's safer for me to go. All right?"

Terje sighed, an inaudible fall of breath. "Regny. I'm going."

"All right," Regny whispered. "All right. Just wait here for me; I'll see if the hunters are still around. All right?"

"Yes."

He stood motionless, trying to hear Regny's movements through the forest, unsurprised when he couldn't. His thoughts turned to Kyreol. He resisted an impulse to look at the sky to see if an interplanetary vessel might by chance be passing overhead. Xtal. He tried to remember what he had learned about it. Second planet from the sun, smallest in the system, full of volcanic dust and sulphur, and some of the most advanced underground cities in the system. Most of what he remembered, she had told him, her face alight with wonder and curiosity. Much of the time when she talked of other worlds, he didn't listen. He watched her face, its constantly varying expressions making him smile. Now he wished he had listened. But even as he concentrated on Xtal, her face drifted among the stars where the planet should have been, and he felt himself smiling again, thinking of all the things she would have to tell him after her long journey. Then two hunters making their way home after their vigil passed him, and he made his mind as quiet as his body. They didn't notice him; they spoke softly, briefly to one another.

"Who will become the new Healer?"

"No one knows."

"The Healer will know before he dies."

"The River will give him a dream."

"The River dreams the World."

They faded away into the night. Terje swallowed, his body suddenly stiff and heavy as a tree trunk, a numbness seeping into his face. For a moment he thought he couldn't move. Then he was moving, very quickly but noiselessly, trying to breathe around the weight in his chest. If there were other hunters, he didn't see them. His mind was focused on the frail, wavering flame within the dark house. He reached it finally, sweating and beginning to tremble, though he hadn't run far. He hugged the stones, eased his face into one of the open windows.

A roil of smoke full of pungent herbs almost made him cough. Then the air cleared, and he could make out the firelit figures. A woman—Korre's mother—sat beside the firepit, crushing dried herbs into it between her fingers. The Healer lay beneath furs. His eyes were closed. The fire swam across his face, and Terje could see the sweat, the deep furrows of pain. Icrane made a sudden, restive movement as Terje gazed at him, turning his head, murmuring, and the woman put her hand quickly to his brow.

Terje sank down under the window. His mouth was dry; he tried to swallow but couldn't. His eyes stung from the smoke. "I can't even talk to him," he heard himself whisper. "I can't even tell him—" And then Regny was there, his steady hold coaxing Terje up from the ground, his face hard, stunned in the light.

"Go," he breathed. They moved far downriver, past the houses, deep into the forest before they spoke again.

They stopped on a sandy, boulder-strewn bank. The great broken stones would hide their fire; the water, running swiftly there, would hide their voices. Terje gathered twigs, struck firestones over them aimlessly, but they refused to spark, and Regny, with a muttered exclamation, took them out of his hands.

"Flint." The sudden exasperation in his voice made Terje stare at him. Regny struck a fire and added harshly to the flame, "One call to the Outstation, Domecity could send medication—"

"No."

Regny looked at him. The anger left his face. He added twigs to the fire and said softly, "The River is the World."

"Yes." The word caught in his throat, hurt. He said unsteadily, "I wonder—I wonder what's the matter with him."

"Snake bite. Food poisoning. Some virus."

"Was it us? Kyreol and me? Leaving him?" He stirred away from the thought. "I heard some hunters talking. He doesn't have— He never chose anyone to teach his healings to. Maybe he thought Kyreol would come back."

"After four years, he would hardly be dying of sorrow."

"He—he should have known."

"He should have known what?"

"That he would need to choose the next Healer."

"He's not that old. He probably didn't expect this."

Terje picked up a twig, burrowed holes in the sand with it, searching for words. "This is one of the things he should have dreamed," he said finally. Regny was silent; Terje added, burrowing deep, "He is probably expecting Kyreol. And she's on Xtal."

Regny sighed. "I don't know. Maybe. You know this world better than I do. But I really don't think, with all his powers of dreaming and foresight, he would spend his dying hours expecting someone who isn't going to come."

Terje's hand stilled. He tossed the twig on the fire,

swept his hair back with his hands, his face bewildered. "She'll be angry with herself," he said softly.

"She couldn't have come here even if she had known."

"She'll be angry that she ever left. That her father is dying and she's on another planet."

"These things happen," Regny said gently.

"Not very often," Terje said, sighing, "in the Riverworld."

He was silent then, gazing into the fire, his body assuming a hunter's pose, unremarkable as a stone. Memories of the Healer ran through his mind: childhood memories of Icrane standing beneath torch-fire on the betrothal carpet, of Icrane gazing at the Moon-Flash, of him in a boat at midnight, holding fire and water, chanting the names of the dead to the River. And earlier memories, of Icrane and Nara, before she had left him to find the River's end. Of Icrane and Nara and a very small Kyreol, gathering herbs and bark for dream tea in the forest. Of Icrane opening the door to Terje's knock, his face at once fierce and gentle, a peaceful man, a dreamer of mysteries, whose voice was the River's voice, whose mind was the World.

The fire formed under his eyes again. Regny was gone; he had slipped away quietly, probably to hunt, for dawn was breaking and the small animals would be stirring. But he didn't come back for hours. Terje caught a fish, then prowled the forest for berries. His prowling led him upriver. He watched the Healer's house from under brush-cover. The Riverworld seemed to be going about its accustomed habits.

People brought small gifts to the Healer's doorstep: food, flowers, a caged bird. But there was no gathering of boats by day. The scented smoke still drifted out of the roof, hung in the still trees.

He found Regny again in the late afternoon, dozing in the sunlight on the sand. He lifted his head as Terje sat down beside him.

"Where did you go?" Terje asked.

"Outstation."

"Why?"

Regny swept sand out of his hair, yawning. "Nara." "What?"

He sat up, blinking. "Nara," he said again, his eyes on the whorling, dimpling water. "She seemed uneasy when we left. Maybe this was why. I thought she should know that the Healer is so ill." He paused, added, "She said you could return to Domecity when you wanted to. I'll stay."

"I'm all right," Terje said.

"I told her that." He pitched a stone into the water. "She sounded—not surprised. But very sad."

"They've been leaving gifts at his door all day."

"It's hard for her." He threw another stone, with more force. "She makes the rules. She could save his life, probably. But—"

"I understand," Terje said, looking away from him.

"I don't," Regny breathed. "Sometimes I really don't." He skipped a piece of flint halfway across the River. "She loved him, she married him, she's not permitted to do anything, even see him. She said she's glad you're here."

"Why?" Terje said.

"Because you're part of both her worlds. You know the Healer. You're part of her early memories. Of when she was young and lived happily with Icrane and had no idea anything at all existed beyond the Riverworld. You can share her sorrow. She also said don't do anything stupid."

"Oh."

"She said impulsive. I say stupid."

"I won't," Terje said mechanically. Regny looked at him. His face eased suddenly.

"You understand this world so well. This tiny, peculiar Riverworld."

Terje nodded absently. "It's easy to understand. You sit quietly, listening to the River, and after a while everything in the Riverworld—even death—becomes just part of everything else. Everything changes, nothing changes. You see it—through the dream. To someone from Domecity, it's just a tiny stretch of water some primitive people happen to be living along. But to someone in the dream, every leaf and every child is exactly right. Exactly as it must be. They'd have to dream an enormous dream to understand Domecity." He drew his eyes away from the water, added softly, "So. I won't do anything stupid. It's not only Domecity that makes the rules. The Riverworld does, too. I don't think it would like them broken."

They stood watch again that night along with the other hunters. Torch-fire crusted the water; the chanting began again. Birds called through the trees, wakened from their sleep. Terje found himself dozing on his feet and realized that he hadn't slept for two days. He let Regny watch for him and lay down under a tree. He thought longingly of Kyreol, remembering, during their long journey downriver, how she was always there when he woke. They had told each other their dreams . . . He fell asleep, remembering. When he woke hearing his name, he thought she was calling him. He lifted his head, murmuring, confused, smelling the damp earth.

"Terje!"

His breath froze. Regny was shaking him, but it wasn't Regny's voice.

A woman's voice. The Healer's door was open; light spilled down the bank and into the water.

"Terje!" she called again, her voice soft, deep, unsurprised. He got to his feet, staring in horror at Regny, trying to see his dark face in the dark.

"No one saw me," he whispered. "I swear it, Regny, no one saw me—"

"Terje!"

"What should I do?"

"Terje! The Healer wants you! Come!"

"Regny—"

Regny's warning grip finally eased on his arm. "Well," he said, his breathing quick, "when you're in a simple world, do the simplest thing possible."

"Terje!"

"Answer her."

4

KYREOL OPENED her eyes. For a moment she only saw darkness and the memory of a fading dream . . . *What was it? Night, water, torch-fire, something to do with Terje, something sad.* Her throat burned with a deep, inexplicable sorrow. "Terje," she whispered and, turning her head, felt the tears brush off fabric in front of her face. She was enveloped, as if between two soft, giant hands; she was surrounded. She struggled and light fell over her face.

She gave a startled, helpless sob, remembering. They had fallen out of the sky; a world of pure white hurtled itself at them, growing larger and larger. She pummeled the softness around her; it gave, and she crawled out onto ripped metal, cracked and melted shielding. Two of the air-beds had torn free, sandwiched themselves around her. *The ship didn't explode*, she thought surprisedly. *Maybe we're all right.* But she heard no voices. Only wind, and the tiny tick of sand blowing into the hull.

Still on her hands and knees, she felt her eyes swell again with tears. A hand lay across her vision, motionless, waxen. She reached out, swallowing, and felt for a pulse. She made her head turn finally to look at the face. It was the navigator.

The pilot still sat strapped to her chair, her face against the control panel. She had salvaged what she could of the landing; the ship was battered and ruined, but upright. She had dragged it across the unknown landscape, slowed it enough to save Kyreol's life.

"Joss Tappan," Kyreol whispered. The silence within and without was dead. She drew breath and screamed, "Joss!"

Hours later, she huddled in a blanket outside the ship, watching the sky. It was night; the moon had turned its back to the sun. The fretful wind had finally died. Moons, half-moons, quarter-moons were suspended in a breathtaking serenity above her, striped light and dark by the sun's fire, the planet's shadow. Of the eighteen moons, she had no idea which one she was on.

"I should remember," she said reasonably to the protrusion of rock she sat on. "It's the one I can breathe on." After the hour she had spent weeping, searching the ship for Joss, trying the dead controls, it had finally occurred to her that whatever else was amiss, the atmosphere was breatheable.

Still she hadn't found Joss. One of three things might have happened:

He had fallen out as they bumped and crashed across the moon's surface.

He had been dazed and wandered off, leaving the wind to cover his footprints in the soft, white sand.

One of his alien friends had spirited him away to an underground cavern, where even now he was instructing them to find Kyreol.

"Someone on the planet must have seen the crash," she murmured hopefully, gazing at the violet edge of planet among the moons. "A tiny moon-flash of exhaust . . ."

But what kind of people lived in Niade's water? Could they even make ships? Did they even see the stars? The planet was a mist of blue, marbled with a white and lavender cloud-cover. It was, she remembered, beautiful and dangerous . . .

She pulled another thermal blanket around her, wondering how long night was. She wouldn't freeze; she wouldn't go hungry. She had salvaged food, water out of a broken line, blankets. She had put on a spacesuit to shield herself from the dust, though it was bulky and uncomfortable with all its tubes, communicators, protective systems. The blankets felt more comforting. She wanted a fire, but in the barren, white landscape, there was nothing to burn.

There were no colors.

"No colors," she said softly. If she couldn't find anyone else to talk to, then she'd talk to the rock. "Black and white. And the black is only shadow . . ."

Later, she ate something out of a tube, drank a bit of the water she had carefully drained from the tank. Then she lay down, bundled in all the blankets she had found, yet still cold. And as lonely as if she were the last person in the universe.

"Terje," she whispered, curling up into a ball. But he was on the other side of night and space. So far away all she could do was send him a dream. *Terje* . . .

★

SUNLIGHT ROLLED the darkness back across the moon's face, and Kyreol saw the city.

It was white. It lay just on the curve of the horizon, a vast, single slab of stone rising out of the moon's bedrock, carved into clusters of ovals, blocks, bubbles, thin, towering cylinders. In the bright light, parts of it glowed like white fire.

Kyreol stood up slowly, shedding blankets. The city was a dream, a lovely illusion sparked by the white dust and the sun's rays. Or maybe any moment a bubble would open; a spacecraft elegant and white as eggshell would appear . . . Perhaps Joss had seen it, had gone there. But was it real? She watched, shading her eyes against the sun. The vision didn't melt away. It was real. But no ship appeared.

Nothing seemed to move around it at all.

Well, she decided after a while. *Maybe it's a factory, not a space-city.*

But even then there would be ships. Freighters, shuttles . . . The sky was motionless, empty above the city.

"Well, maybe it's just a city." Her voice sounded high, frightened to her ears. She had never encountered an alien from Niade before, never even seen a photograph of one. She had only met three aliens in her entire life, and these on the Observers' Deck in the Dome with Joss Tappan beside her. They had been trade officials, who spoke the language of the Dome.

"It's a city full of people who don't go anywhere. In which case," she asked herself, "how did they get here on this moon?"

They had always been here. A pale, dry, dusty people, like their surroundings, whose eyes were made to see only one color.

She had to watch it a long time, the silent, sparkling city, while she argued with herself, before she finally found the courage to go to it.

I should stay here, guard the ship.

From what? she asked herself.

Someone from the Dome might come looking for us. I'm safe here; I have food, water.

How would the Dome know where you crashed? There may not have been time to send a message.

Maybe there was time.

It will take them nearly three days to get here. If they know where you are. The people in that city might be able to communicate with the Dome. Maybe the Dome knows where you are, but what if it doesn't? You could wait here for three days for a ship that isn't coming. Meanwhile, Nara will worry—

"She felt something like this would happen." Kyreol interrupted herself, surprised. "For that matter, so did I."

Anyway, she added to herself, *what about Joss Tappan? What if he comes here?*

Joss Tappan isn't afraid of alien cultures. He'd go to the city. He may already be there.

Kyreol's eyes went to the torn, broken hull of the

ship. The powdery sand was already packing against it. A piece of torn fabric fluttered within, then was still. "What," she whispered, "about the dead?"

Her argumentative voice, suddenly silent, offered no advice. Water, earth, deep space—these things accepted the dead. But here, there was only the dry dust of an alien world. Kyreol scooped up a handful of it, frowning, and let it sift through her fingers.

"They need to go home," she decided finally. "Meanwhile—"

Her eyes burning, her jaw set hard against her loneliness and fear, she covered them as best she could, shielding them from the sand and the unfamiliar night. Then she shed the spacesuit and filled a backpack with food and water, extra clothes, a com-crystal, a laser, and odd things that looked useful: a piece of thick wire, a table knife, a bar of soap, a tiny tape recorder, a book she had been reading, her comb, a feather amulet Nara had given her for luck, a nose-filter and a pair of goggles, and a light, voluminous raincoat that could double as a tent if the dust storms became impossible. The pack, fat as a sausage, dragged at her shoulder. *This is stupid*, she thought. *I can walk to the city in a couple of hours*. But still she took the pack.

The city was much bigger and farther than she had guessed. It grew very slowly as she toiled toward it. She stopped to eat finally, studied it while she chewed. A few hours later, she had to stop again, as the white city melted into a hazy, purple twilight. She woke groggily in the morning, sore and dusty. Still nothing moved in the bright city, or in the sky, or in the land around it.

Were they people, like the Burrowers, who couldn't bear light?

No, she decided finally. *People sensitive to light did not build cities under a hot sun.*

Then what? She swallowed drily, uneasy with the thought that crossed her mind. She shouldered her pack again and rose.

Finally she reached the edge of the great shadow spilling across the bone-dry ground. She stopped, tired, sweating, her face pale with dust and stared up at the sheer bluff of stone. Then she looked down at her feet.

No other footprints.

She slid her hands over her mouth, suddenly panicked, preferring aliens to the chilly silence of the city's emptiness.

"There must be someone!" she whispered. "There must be!"

She began to walk again, doggedly, into the shadow.

The city was like nothing she had ever seen. Massive yet translucent, like the Dome, it had been built with an astonishing degree of sophistication. Stairways wandered up and down the walls; chambers she thought might be elevators clung to various levels like bubbles. The great domes and cylinders must house generators, power plants, factories, air docks. If the people who built the city had traveled by land, their roads had long been buried under the dust. Perhaps they were an air-faring people, preferring the sky to the barren land, preferring the security of their walls to the restless wind and harsh storms.

But where had they come from? Not from the water-planet, surely; the people there had no concept of cities. They lived in a fluid, shifting environment; they wouldn't imagine a city resting on a flat, still surface. Still, if they had such a dream, it might look something like this: delicate, light-filled, shapes clustered together like bubbles in foam.

She reached the outer wall. An elevator hung over her head. She pushed a dusty button beside a stairway. Nothing happened. Looking closer, she saw the white stairs had been built to move. They moved no longer; dust must have choked their mechanisms long ago. Dust lay undisturbed; nothing had climbed them recently but the sun.

She began to climb. She plunged from light into shadow. She counted two hundred steps, then stopped counting. Would anyone of a water-world build all those steps? She was tempted to remove her pack, but she was afraid of forgetting where she had left it. Finally she found a door. It was round, convex, like a half-bubble. And it was partly open.

She peered inside.

Hundreds and hundreds of white rods of varying shape and size hung suspended from the ceiling of the room. Kyreol stared at them, her mouth open. Eggs, she decided finally. Alien eggs. The rods were motionless, dusty. She reached out eventually, after a long time, and touched one with the tips of her fingers. It hummed slightly, then fell like a ripe fruit ready to drop at a breeze, and shattered to pieces on the floor.

She fell against the door in horror, hiding her face in her hands. The sound clanged in her ears. Then the silence fell again, smothering, cloying, like the dust.

She wiped tears off her face, felt the mask of powder on it. That made her more miserable. *I'll stay here and get buried like everything else.* Then she thought, *Maybe they're not eggs. Maybe it's a kind of . . . a kind of . . .*

What?

An energy source? A library? An information storage? Part of a vast computer?

"If there's a computer, maybe there's a communications system," she said aloud. "Maybe I can call the Dome. If I can find it. If I can recognize it. If it still works." She moved among the rods, feeling her mind starting to work again. "Maybe there's a little air shuttle. I can fly it above the surface and look for Joss." She reached another bubble door. It opened easily, melting in half into the wall. "What kind of people would have built fat round doors?"

Bubble-people. They rolled from room to room. She laughed suddenly at her own invention. The laugher echoed into silence.

The next room was a vast, domed area. It was full of huge white cylinders and ovals, each with softly translucent screens and what looked like a code system of lights. But none of the lights burned. The main computer? she guessed, remembering the one in the Dome that constantly told her she was doing something wrong. She glanced behind her abruptly, terrified of getting lost within the city. Her footprints marched behind her without a break.

"I'll find a shuttle," she whispered, then. "I'll find Joss." An airship she might possibly fly; the computer was too formidable. "I don't know enough," she protested tightly. "I'm too ignorant for this."

She crossed the huge room, opened another bubble-door. This room, too, was full of rods. But they were different: heavier, crystal-clear, prismed. Late sunlight struck them through a window; a membrane of color trembled in the air like a butterfly wing.

Someone was singing.

Kyreol's knees buckled; she sat down in the dust. Her mouth dried; her heart seemed to leap up and down on her stomach. The voice roamed aimlessly from tone to tone; sometimes it buzzed like a bee, sometimes it sounded like a high-pitched stringed instrument. Whoever owned it was coming closer.

A shadow loomed across the bubble-door. Kyreol shut her eyes. She heard the door open. The singing wailed upward into a high, loud, wobbly note, as something shuffled inside.

Half a dozen rods, vibrating overtones, crashed to the ground and splintered.

The singer gave a yip of shock. Kyreol buried her face in her knees and screamed.

Silence fell once again over the city.

5

THE HEALER lay in a restless weave of smoke, fire, shadow. Terje, stepping slowly into the small room, smelled herbs again, and some sweetly burning wood and, beneath that, the Healer's sweat. He was lying quietly. His face was much thinner than Terje remembered. His eyes were closed. The woman beckoned to Terje, made him sit on the carpet beside the bed. Her eyes, preoccupied until then, stayed on Terje's face in sudden curiosity. Her son, Korre, had been betrothed to Kyreol. Kyreol had left him, had vanished completely with Terje. And here was Terje, four Moon-Flashes later, come back out of nowhere, dressed as a hunter, yet telling no one he had returned.

He was a dream, a ghost. The Healer had called him up from the dead. She touched him tentatively as he sat gazing at the Healer. He turned, startled. The sadness, the confusion in his expression, the sweat already gathering on his face, the smudges of sleeplessness under his eyes told her he was no ghost. A boy had gone somewhere; a young man had returned.

But from where?

She asked nothing; that was for the Healer to do. Instead, she put a cup of tea in Terje's hands. He drank it mechanically. It was scalding and very bitter. Some protection against fever, perhaps. As soon as he set the cup down, though, he felt disoriented, almost as if he were watching himself from one of the shadows. A dream-tea. The Healer's eyes opened. He looked at Terje silently, his dark eyes expressionless, unblinking, until Terje felt all his memories of the past years become as a dream in his head, a curious story. The Riverworld was the real world.

He drew a deep breath, knowing that all of Nara's careful rules and regulations meant nothing in this situation. The Healer's mind had reached out into the darkness and found him, in spite of all Terje's skill and training. He was a dying man. Those he had loved most in the world had left him without a trace. Only Terje had returned.

He has a right, Terje said silently, stubbornly, to Regny, to Nara, to all the agents who were even now moving in secret, in primitive disguises, among the tiny, ancient cultures of the world. *He has a right to truth.*

The Healer's face softened; his eyes smiled faintly. Terje asked surprisedly, "Are you hearing my thoughts?"

"Just the thoughts on your face." He lifted one hand, patted Terje's arm weakly. "I'm glad you came back."

44

Terje swallowed. He touched the Healer's cheek briefly with the back of his fingers. It was very hot. "What happened?" he asked huskily. "What's making you sick?"

"Something from the air." He closed his eyes briefly, his brow furrowing. *Fever*, Terje thought. It might have been anything—virus, insect bite, bacteria from the water. Children were more prone to unidentified fevers; in adults, they were rare and deadly.

The Healer's fingers tightened on his arm, bringing Terje out of his thoughts. Icrane's eyes were wide open again. He looked past Terje, to Korre's mother.

"You must go now," he said to her gently. "For a little while. Terje will tell me what he has been dreaming for so long."

Korre's mother rose reluctantly. She wiped the sweat from the Healer's face, then gave the cloth to Terje, whispering, "I won't go far. Call if he needs help."

Terje nodded. The door opened; the smoke swirled, then drew once more toward the roof. The Healer frowned again, more in bewilderment than pain.

"Where did you go, Terje? I have had such strange dreams of you and Kyreol. I knew you were alive. Like Nara. But where is there to go that is not the Riverworld?"

"We went— We followed the River to its end."

"How? Tell me how."

Terje told him how they had gone to see the rainbows at Fourteen Falls and almost killed themselves going down the Falls. How they had met people living in the cliffs beyond the Falls—

The Healer shifted, amazed. "Is this true, Terje? Or did you dream it?"

"It's true," Terje said softly. "Dreams don't kill. We journeyed through the real world, full of fierce people, dangerous animals, the hot desert sun, the River itself . . ."

"Is the world that big?"

"Yes."

"And that strange?"

"It's stranger than anything you could dream."

The Healer shook his head, smiling again. "I've seen that world already, I think. I'm glad you came back to explain my dreams to me."

A weight seemed to sag away from Terje; he leaned forward, bowed his head against the feather pallet, smelling the herbs scattered among the skins. His hands were closed tightly. "I was afraid to tell you . . . We are all afraid."

He felt the Healer's hand on his hair, heard the surprise in his voice. "Is that why I never saw you again? Because you were all afraid?"

"You don't understand."

"Nara? Is that why my wife never returned to me?"

"Yes."

"I think you're right," Icrane said after a moment. "I don't understand. Tell me more. Make me understand."

Terje straightened. He knew he should pick and choose among facts, make them simple, comprehensible, to a simple world. But something in the tea

46

had jumbled everything in his head, made everything at once real and dreamlike, made nothing important except the small stone room, the fire, the Healer, walking toward death, gazing back at life, and wondering at it.

"Are they well?" the Healer asked. "My wife and my daughter?"

"Yes."

"Are you and Kyreol betrothed? You always liked her. I thought at first that was why you ran away."

"No. We—she wouldn't have run away for that. We're not betrothed. Well." He stopped. "In a way, we are."

The Healer nodded. "In spirit. That's important."

"I didn't know you thought that way."

"Rituals don't permit such thoughts. But dreams do . . . I know them both. And Nara?" His voice was suddenly wistful. "Is she bound in spirit also? To someone else?"

Terje shook his head. "I don't think so. I think she left her heart here."

Icrane drew a long, silent breath, loosed it as silently. "Then why," he whispered almost fiercely, "has she never returned? I never stopped thinking of her. She ate my heart like the moon eats the sun."

Terje swallowed. He wiped the Healer's face wordlessly, wishing he could concentrate. All his muscles had tensed again. He wished Regny were with him, guarding his words, telling him how much he should say.

"She—the world is so different, at the end of the River," he heard himself say. "Even the moon is different." He stopped, suddenly frightened. Icrane's eyes were on his face.

"How is the moon different?"

"The Moon-Flash came from that world. The people at the end of the River made the Moon-Flash." He stopped again, floundering in the Healer's silence. "The ritual is different there."

The Healer wasn't breathing. Terje gazed at him, alarmed. The man's eyes were focused on the shadows; soon he gave a soft sigh.

"Boats," he whispered. "Boats among the stars."

Terje's skin prickled. "Yes."

"I dreamed that."

"She thought—she thought that for you to know such things would make you—would change the way you look at the Riverworld. That's why she never came back. She was trying to protect you."

"Ah." Icrane closed his eyes. His face, in the shifting light, seemed easier, more peaceful. Terje turned, added wood to the fire, scattered a handful of herbs from the bowl beside the firebed. "That," he heard Icrane whisper, "I almost understand. Terje."

Terje turned back to him. Icrane opened his eyes; black, still, secret, they caught at Terje and held him. "Why are you here?" Icrane asked. His words were slow, frail. "I felt you here yesterday and the day before. You were in my dreams . . . a silent hunter standing among the trees. Yet no one spoke your name, and you never came to greet me, to tell me of Kyreol. Why? Where is Kyreol? Why isn't she with you?"

"Kyreol—" He had to stop to clear his throat. He felt blood rising in his face as he considered his words, like a man standing on a stone in a rapid, dangerous river, considering which stone to leap to next. "She's on a journey. She's very far away. Even if she dreams of you, she's too far to come to you."

"Too far . . . How far is that?"

"She's—she's beyond the moon."

Icrane gazed at him in wonder. "Kyreol?" He gave a faint laugh, startling Terje. "The River carried her a little farther than she expected . . ." Terje nodded wordlessly. Icrane reached out, brushed the feathers Terje wore. "Did you make this vest here?"

"No."

"Are you a hunter?"

Terje ran his fingers through his hair. "I hunt," he said finally. The Healer was gazing at him again, patiently, waiting for him to stop edging around the question. He scratched his head, wondering what on earth Regny would say to the Healer at this point. Inspiration came to him. "Nara sends me," he said. "In secret, to find out how you are."

"But she won't come herself."

"It's a different world," Terje said helplessly. "It's huge, it's noisy, it's full of sharp edges and very few dreams. The people in it know of the Riverworld. They know how simple and peaceful it is, and they try to protect that peace. They don't want the Riverworld to disappear into the noisy, crowded world."

Icrane lay very still, no longer looking at Terje. "Yes," he whispered. "Yes. Sometimes, I dreamed of

49

that world. I never knew what it was, or where it might be."

"It's at the end of the River."

"And they know of us?"

"Yes."

"How? Do they dream of us?"

"No. They don't dream very well. People just come like me, in secret. To watch. To guard the Riverworld against anything that might change it."

Icrane's eyes went back to Terje. "You."

"That's why I'm here. I didn't—" He shook his head, swallowing at the sudden burn in his throat. "I didn't know you were—I didn't know—"

Icrane was silent for a long time. His eyes were half-closed; he watched the flames, motionless, unblinking. Terje wondered if he were dreaming. He sat still with an effort. All his hunter's tranquility seemed to have left him. He was sweating, half-scorched by the fire; his muscles were cramped from sitting. He felt alternately grieved, appalled by what he was saying, and awed by Icrane's dreams and by his understanding. He wanted to stay by Icrane's side; he wanted to go into the night, keep walking until he forgot everything except the dark, the singing trees, the River's cool touch. He wanted to talk to Regny, and yet he was afraid to tell Regny how much he was explaining to Icrane.

Am I doing what people have spent years being trained not to do? he wondered. *Am I endangering the Riverworld?*

"They've forgotten how to dream," he heard himself say to Icrane. "That's why they want to protect the Riverworld from their world. They want the Riverworld always to remember how to dream. How to see." He couldn't tell if Icrane had heard him. Finally the Healer stirred, whispering for water, and Terje lifted Icrane's head with his arm, held the water-skin so he could drink. The lines on Icrane's face had deepened again; he moved restlessly when Terje loosed him, trying to escape from his pain.

"Kyreol . . ."

Terje leaned over him. "What?" The Healer's fingers gripped him, hard. "Kyreol—"

"What is it?" He was taking quick, dry breaths, staring at Icrane. The Healer made a sudden, harsh noise. He looked as if he were trying to see light in a lightless place. Terje felt the blood run out of his face.

"Icrane!"

"What kind of world have you found," the Healer whispered, "where such things can happen?"

"What happened?" He didn't know he had shouted until Korre's mother put her head in the door, and he saw a shadow that might have been Regny briefly cross a window. Icrane was still again, hardly breathing, his expression harsh, intent. Then, as Terje and Korre's mother watched him, nearly breathless themselves, his face relaxed again and his feverish grip loosened.

"That's all right." He sighed, his eyes closing. "She'll be all right."

Terje turned his head, looked at Korre's mother. He was so shaken, so frightened that she lost some of her own fear and stepped softly into the room.

51

"He must sleep, Terje."

"I know." But as he shifted to stand, Icrane held him again, this time gently.

"No. Don't go. Stay with me. You have so many things to tell me and so few words to say them with. Maybe . . . there aren't enough words in the River-world."

"Kyreol—" His voice trembled.

"She's having many strange dreams. Stay. Sleep beside me, Terje. You comfort me."

Korre's mother put skins on the floor for him. He stretched out, listening to the Healer's breathing. A tear hot as fire rolled across his arm. Then the soft chanting from the River slid him into shoals of sleep.

6

THERE WAS an argument going on in Kyreol's head.

Kyreol. Lift up your head and see what it is.

No.

How can you learn about aliens if you don't look at them?

Nobody said I had to do it alone.

But you are alone. You have to.

No.

Then what are you going to do? Sit here with your eyes closed until you're covered with dust?

It's better than seeing something that might scare me to death.

But, Kyreol—

No.

But—

She lifted her head slightly, peeked out at an angle above her arm, her eye half-hidden by her hair. She blinked. A big ball of iridescent fur leaned against the opposite wall near the door. It seemed to have no head. Where its head should have been, six fingers, rough and pointed like carrots, were interlaced. Two humps with what looked like various tools and instruments belted around them, rose underneath the fingers. Kyreol shifted to look out of both eyes. The humps descended into feet ringed with bright bracelets of fur. In the angle formed by the knees and the feet a single eye, surrounded by a perfect circle of black fur, gazed back at Kyreol.

Kyreol lifted her head slowly. The eye rolled up into the fur. A soft, high note trembled in the air.

She sat up silently, amazed. *It's as scared as I am*, she thought. Her hands felt like ice; her heart was pounding raggedly. *And that's pretty scared. Now what do I do?* She whispered, "Joss, what do I do?"

The creature hummed again, gently, so not to break more rods. Its eye was still hidden. Kyreol, her voice trembling and cracked with terror, hummed the same note back at it.

The eye opened again. The fingers shifted slightly. Something very small and furry bulged briefly underneath the hands. A second eye opened above the first.

It studied Kyreol for a long time, then turned gradually from a pale pink to a deep purple. A third eye opened.

Kyreol jumped, startled. All the eyes disappeared at once.

She sat very still again, terrified and fascinated at the same time. The instruments dangling from the creature's kneebelts looked sleek, complex, the tools of the explorer. But it was using none of them. Not even a communicator to call one of its kind and say:

I'm alone in a room with an alien with a black face and a silver body. It has only two eyes, and they're in the wrong place. Please come— *I'd be doing that,* Kyreol thought, *if I had anyone to call.* She watched another little lump of fur burrow into the deep fur around the shoulders *Will it attack me?* she wondered nervously. *If I stand up? Does it have teeth? Will it shoot me with something?*

One eye opened again, cautiously. A faint, brief hum curled up into the air, like a question. Kyreol tried to imitate it; her voice only squeaked like a mouse.

The creature shifted. All its eyes opened. Its hands unlocked very slowly. As its shoulders lowered, all the vague little movements on them ceased. Its head rose from between its knees.

Its long neck retracted. Its head was a mound of pure white fur. The eyes were ringed with black; the oval pupils were purple. It had no teeth; its mouth was a hard, shiny white beak. The humming came from two moist, mobile slits on the sides of its beak. It sat back against the wall, studying Kyreol out of three eyes. Then the center eye closed. Its hands opened, stroked the small, quivering, brightly colored fur-balls that circled its shoulders and front like a chain. A fine, faint, very high sound, like a musical purr of many tiny voices, drifted up from under its hands.

Kyreol's mouth opened. "Babies?" she breathed, and at the new sound, the long bony fingers stilled.

The eyes paled nervously, but the creature didn't

curl up again. Kyreol smiled, half in wonder, half in relief, and the beak opened in another startled yip.

"Oh please," Kyreol pleaded. "Don't disappear again. Look. I'm not moving. I'm sitting still. It's just me, Kyreol. I'm nothing to be afraid of." All the eyes were closed again. But instead of curling in fear, the being rested its head against the white wall, wailing softly to itself like a mournful, perfectly pitched violin.

Kyreol's fear eased. She sat transfixed, her chin in her hands, wondering how in the world she could talk to something that made noises through its nose like an orchestra. *What is it saying? Probably*: 'What am I doing here on this empty moon, I wish I were home . . .' *But where is its ship? Did it crash like us? If it's so terrified, why is it even here? How can I ask?*

And then, alarmed again, she thought: *Mothers are sometimes dangerous. Will it think I'm a threat if I stand?*

She sat very still, then. They gazed at one another across the room; the creature's eyes paled occasionally at some fearful thought of its own. The younglings stopped moving after a while; they looped their parent's neck in a bright, lumpy chain. *Napping*, Kyreol thought, and sighed. *Now what? I'm here, it's there, we can't talk to each other, and neither one of us is going to move. What if it bites?* Space explorers, she knew, usually didn't bite other aliens. But if it was an explorer, why was it so frightened?

It was moving. It lifted one bony hand from the ring of young, held it out. Its fingers closed, uncurled.

Closed, uncurled. An alien greeting? Kyreol lifted her hand very carefully. The alien fingers curled, uncurled. One finger at a time.

One. Two. Three.

"Oh," she breathed, and opened her own fingers. "One." Her voice sounded peculiar in the dead air, still shaking, and high as a child's. "Two. Three. Four. Five."

Then she waited, her mouth open in astonishment, while the creature went through an amazing confusion of sounds. First the white beak clicked, a brittle, insect-sound. Then the beak-vents made noises like a steam whistle, a windstorm, a tree full of monkeys, a horn, a bass drum, a pool of boiling mud, a window breaking, a foghorn, the beginning of a symphony, and finally, a ghostly voice that vaguely resembled Kyreol's, saying: "One."

Kyreol stared at it, stunned. It held one finger up. Its beak made a brief series of clicks, like a code. One, Kyreol thought after a moment. One. Her mouth was still hanging open. She closed it. The only thing she had to click with was her teeth, and the beak noises were far too rapid. The alien finger closed after a moment. They gazed at one another again perplexedly.

It had no eyebrows, Kyreol realized. Where her own face was mobile with expression, the furry, beaked face could only change its eye color. No wonder it had been startled when she smiled.

Now what? she thought again. *Here we are, two aliens stuck in a dead city on a strange moon. How can we talk?* Then she stared down at the dust on the floor.

Pictures.

She stood up. The creature mourned a little, but its eyes didn't close. She walked slowly, noiselessly, to the center of the room. There, with a clearer sense of the size of the alien, her courage faltered. *No closer*, its silence seemed to warn. *No closer*. She knelt down and began to draw.

"This is the sun." Her voice wobbled in the still air. "These are the seven planets. Corios. Xtal. Niade." She drew large circles with her forefinger, so that the alien could see them where it sat. "Thanos, Chance, Tliklok, Septa. One, two, three, four, five, six, seven. I am from Thanos." She pointed to herself, then at the planet. "Four." She added a moon. Then she pointed to the third planet. "Three." She surrounded that one with moons. "Niade. Number Three. This is where we are now. On one of its moons." Her hand swept over them. She sat back, shrugging. "I don't know which one."

The creature's eye had turned an even deeper purple. It made some rapid clicks. Then it rose, about seven feet, making Kyreol's heart turn over. From its knee-belt, it selected a small instrument. *What have I said?* Kyreol thought wildly. *It's going to shoot me.* But it pointed the instrument at the wall it had been leaning against. The wall flushed blue-black, patterned with an icy swirl of stars.

"A star map," Kyreol breathed. The forefinger made a shadow across the map, pointing to a sun. Then it pointed at Kyreol. *Your sun.* The shadow shifted to a neighboring star, bigger, with a bluish glow. It tapped the top of its white mound. *Mine*, the tap said.

Kyreol swallowed drily, frozen on the floor.

"You're not even from this system."

7

TERJE WOKE suddenly under a shaft of light. The door was open; he saw Korre's mother, bending over the river, filling skins. He looked at the Healer. He seemed to be sleeping quietly; his breathing was soft and slow. Terje sat up, memories of the previous night jumbled in his head along with his dreams. Things he had told the Healer came back to him. Or had he only dreamed of saying them? He wished, fervently, that he had. He felt bone tired. The smell of earth, herbs, wood smoke stirred older memories in him. He watched needles of dancing light on the water through the open doorway, listened to the distant, daily noises of the Riverworld. Children swimming, women calling to one another across the water . . .

I'm home, he thought, strangely satisfied. Then he remembered Kyreol and the Healer's vision of her, and the frail peace vanished. He got to his feet, wanting the warmth of the morning. Korre's mother returned. She smiled and handed him some nut-bread and berries for breakfast.

"I'll be back," he whispered to her. "Tell him, when he wakes. I won't be gone long."

He kept to the thick parts of the forest, wanting to avoid questions, heading downriver toward the hidden campsite. Birds called brightly, soared through the light around him. He felt, for a little while, that he could simply disappear into his hunter's role, treat the Dome as a dream, become Terje of the Riverworld, eating berries and fish and worrying about nothing. Except the Healer. And Kyreol. And how to go on being an unobserved observer when most of the Riverworld must have heard his name called into the night . . .

And Regny.

He found Regny at their hidden camp, sitting on a rock with a line in the water. His steps were soundless on the warm sand; Regny looked up, startled, as Terje's shadow fell over him. Terje sat down beside him.

"How is he?" Regny asked.

"He's sleeping. Regny—"

"Nothing's biting this morning, and I'm starving."

"Try some turtle eggs. Regny—" His voice stuck. He sighed and found it again. "I think I just broke every rule I was ever taught."

"I know you did," Regny said calmly.

"How much did you hear?"

"Everything." He began coiling his line and added, "The Healer broke a few rules himself. He wasn't supposed to know from his dreams you were here. He wasn't supposed to send someone to call out your name in front of the entire Riverworld. And he cer-

tainly wasn't supposed to be dreaming about space-
ships."

"He dreamed about Kyreol."

"I know. I heard you shout. Did he say what—"

"No." He dug absently in the sand. "I'll ask him
again today, if he's well enough to talk. Is Nara
going to be angry with me?"

Regny smiled a little. "She'll be grateful you are
here. This business of us sneaking around in feathers
while people from the Riverworld are flying around
in space and dreaming of the Dome is getting a little
incongruous. And we could cure the Healer."

Terje looked at him. "Do you want me to tell him
that?" he asked. His voice was sharp with a sudden
confusion. "The Agency tells me one thing. You tell
me another. Am I supposed to decide whether he
lives or dies? I can't do it, Regny, I just can't. This
isn't the Dome, it's the Riverworld—death is as much a
part of life as dreams here. At least, the Healer be-
lieves that. Do you want me to tell him it's not true?"

"No." Regny sighed. "No." He put his hand on
Terje's shoulder. "I'm sorry. I was just sounding off
at the Agency, not you. It's certainly not a decision for
you to make. You've had to make far too many already." He paused, his eyes on Terje's weary face.
"You can go back to the Dome, you know. Nobody
expected you to have to go through this."

Terje shook his head. "I couldn't leave him," he
said softly. He folded his arms across his knees and
brooded, gazing at the swift green water. He thought
of Kyreol, missed her; he wanted her arms around
him, passing her strength to him through her bones

62

and her thoughts. "I wonder what's happening to her?" he whispered. Regny took river weed from his hook and cast his line out again.

"I don't know," he said grimly. "But as soon as I get some breakfast, I'm making another trip to the Outstation. If anyone knows what's happening on Xtal, Nara will know. I'll make it back to the Healer's house sometime in the night. So if you need me, check outside."

"She was right to send you," Terje said suddenly, looking at Regny. "She was right. I'd be terrified without you."

He returned to the Healer's house at midmorning. The Healer was awake, stirring uneasily; when Terje entered, though, he smiled. His face had a shadowy-gray cast, and he shivered, in spite of the fire and the thick furs over him.

"I'm glad you weren't a dream," he said.

"No," Terje said. "I'm here." He sat down beside the pallet. Icrane quieted, gazing into his face almost curiously, as though he could see the end of the River and the Dome in Terje's eyes. Korre's mother, stirring broth over the fire, crouched down, as unobtrusively as possible. Icrane glanced at her, as if he could feel her listening. But he let her stay.

"Tell me more," he said to Terje, "about your strange dreaming in the world at the end of the River. What kinds of rituals do they have? Do they have a Healer to explain their dreams?"

They don't have rituals, Terje thought. *They don't have a Healer and they don't explain dreams*. He groped through his memories, trying to find something that might seem like a ritual, so that the Healer wouldn't worry about Kyreol living in a place unsuitable for human beings.

He told the Healer how he and Kyreol studied every day, about how they got their food, since there were no hunters, about rituals for births and death and miscellaneous things, like a first moon flight. He couldn't tell how much the Healer understood. His eyes never moved from Terje's face, but he seemed to be thinking more of something behind Terje's words: the tone of his voice, or the expressions in his eyes.

"Are you content there?" the Healer asked simply. Terje paused, realizing that he hadn't asked himself that in a long time. The Dome was the Dome; it didn't offer contentment, but challenges. It paid little attention to dreams, but it had opened his eyes to the endless shapes of reality.

"Kyreol is there," he answered finally. "It's the place we came to, together." They had learned too much; there was no turning back.

"You don't long for the Riverworld?"

"Sometimes," Terje admitted.

"I look in your eyes and see the River flowing there," Icrane whispered. He put his hand over his own eyes suddenly, withdrawing from the light, and turned, uneasy with pain. Korre's mother came to his side.

"He needs to sleep now," she said gently. "You go. But not too far."

Terje went outside to sit on the bank where the Healer's boat was moored. There were children fishing downriver, diving off their small boat, splashing one another. Women washing clothes glanced in his direction, but didn't call to him. A fisherman poling upriver nodded to him, but didn't speak. They viewed him with great courtesy and a little fear, as if he were a visiting ghost. What his coming meant no one knew, but no one dared ask. He was the Healer's business.

Korre's mother came out, stood beside him.

"He's dreaming," she said. She didn't seem to be afraid of Terje any more. He was the same Terje, only four years older, who had sat glowering at Kyreol's betrothal to her son, and who had at last run away with her. Where he had returned from she couldn't imagine; she only knew that he was too distressed to be a ghost and that the Healer valued his presence.

Terje looked up at her. "Will he die?"

Her eyes narrowed slightly; she gazed down at the water.

"A day or two perhaps . . ." she said softly. "He is more peaceful now that you've come."

Terje swallowed. He frowned down at his reflection, feeling hollow, disoriented in the placid afternoon. The Riverworld without Icrane seemed impossible.

"Who will—who will take his place?"

She shrugged slightly, unconcerned. "The Healer will know." She touched his shoulder, patted it comfortingly, as if he were one of her children. "Come and have some soup."

Later in the afternoon, after the Healer had wakened and drunk a strong, soothing tea, Terje asked him about Kyreol. He didn't answer for a moment;

he gazed at the fire, his thoughts straying into some dream-memory.

"Kyreol . . ."

"What happened to her?"

"I saw her flying . . . through the stars. And suddenly, a star fell out of the sky and struck her and she fell . . . There was great fear, terror . . ."

"But she's all right," Terje breathed.

"Yes . . ." The lines of his face puckered slightly, at some curious vision. "I don't understand the things I see. They're like pictures drawn by a strange people. But she is moving among them. Kyreol of the Riverworld . . ." He made a soft noise, half laughter, half wonder. Then his eyes came back from the distance and he looked at Terje.

"Talk to me. Tell me more about your journey down the River. What other things did you see beyond Fourteen Falls?"

So Terje told him about the long gold desert, the marvelous animals that roamed it, about the great, grim stone faces rising out of the river reeds, and the bones that had fallen at Kyreol's feet as she traced the story carved on the back of one of the stern faces. That made the Healer chuckle again, though he seemed surprised at the ritual.

"How strange to lock the dead in stone . . ."

It was as if he were listening to a marvelous story. Terje didn't know how much he believed, if any of it. He told the Healer about the boy with the bells, the desert-child, kin to the Moon, and about the man sent by the Dome to help them on their journey. He intended to say no more about Regny than that, but at the mention of his name, a spark of recognition flashed in the Healer's eyes. He touched Terje's wrist, stopping him.

"Yes . . . I've seen him many times."

Terje stared at him. "Regny?"

"At rituals . . . I see him standing at the edge of the firelight, or alone among the trees. For years I thought he was a ghost, the hunter who wandered so quietly, unexpectedly, in and out of the Riverworld. He didn't mean for me to see him, so I never disturbed him. He was part of the River's dreaming." He added, "So the River's end sent him to guide you and Kyreol."

Terje nodded mutely. He thought how horrified Regny would be, knowing that his presence had been secretly tolerated by the Healer for years. "How did— how did you know Regny wasn't one of the River-world hunters?"

"I know," the Healer said simply. "He looked no different from anyone. But when I saw him, he always made my eyes pause. Something . . . Maybe it was his thoughts. They must have been different from Riverworld thoughts, like a strange sound in a forest."

"He's here now," Terje said abruptly. It seemed useless to hide anything from the Healer.

"So . . . he guided you back to the Riverworld." He was silent then, for so long that Terje thought he had gone to sleep with his eyes open. Korre's mother, sewing a betrothal shirt for one of her daughters, glanced at him anxiously now and then, but his face was untroubled, his eyes as remote as if he were sitting on the moon and thinking. Terje rose after a while, wandering outside, back down to the water. The sun was about to set; long, pale fingers of light stroked the ground. He could smell supper being cooked: fish, onion soup. He heard a baby crying, the birds singing the sun down. The moon had already risen; it hung like a faint, ghostly face in the wake of dying light. The brief, golden days, the nut harvests, the autumn star patterns; he felt the urge toward ritual, a childhood habit, and a habit as old as the history of the Riverworld. Even in the Dome he had felt it, he realized suddenly. He still kept coming back at ritual time; he had found a job that permitted him to return, like a ghost himself, drawn by the ancient patterns of his heritage.

His thoughts strayed to Kyreol; he wished he could have the Healer's dreams. Even more he wished she were here, safe and happy, sitting on the bank with him, counting shooting stars and telling of her adventures. His throat ached suddenly. Before he could see her again, there must be a death. He wished Regny were back.

He turned away from the River, went back into the house. The Healer's eyes went to his face as he entered. He looked very tired, in pain again, but his eyes were peaceful. He gestured weakly; Terje knelt in the furs at his side.

"Terje . . . I had a dream."

"About Kyreol?" he asked hopefully.

"No. It was about you. You held the great River in one hand and the Moon-Flash in your other hand . . ." He paused, swallowing. Korre's mother was still; even the twigs on the fire were still. Terje felt his neck hair prickle. He wanted to draw back from the Healer, but the deep black gaze bound him motionless. "It was a good dream," the Healer said tranquilly. "One I have been waiting for. It was the dream of a new Healer. The River has chosen you."

8

THE WHITE CITY revolved into night. Kyreol, curled up in the raincoat on the dusty floor, listened to the alien humming its young to sleep. The humming was deep, bass, meandering softly from note to note. In the dark, it was a soothing sound, like the voice of a river . . .

She woke abruptly, sweating in hot light. Images from a dream tumbled away from her; she caught at them: the first dream she had remembered in a long time, clear and bright with color. Terje. Terje with his hair blazing like sunlight. He had picked up the River in one hand, like a wide blue ribbon. On his forehead was the Moon-Flash. In his other hand was . . . *what?* Kyreol sat up, not seeing anything, intent on the scattering impressions. *What was in his other hand?* She remembered then, and frowned, puzzled, but the dream had spoken.

A stone face. He held one of the great, gaunt black stone faces they had passed on their journey downriver.

She swallowed, feeling her heartbeat. The blank eyes gazed at her from Terje's head, sightless yet seeing . . .

"Terje?" she said tremulously to the air. Tears gathered in her eyes, fell, for as vast as the night was between them Terje had reached across it to tell her something, and the stone face was the message.

Death, a tiny voice in her mind said. She made a sound, wiping at her face, and an echo of the sound came at her from across the room.

She jumped, remembering the alien. It was peering at her out of all three eyes. Its young were awake, roaming around its shoulders; Kyreol could hear their high, rambling melodies. The alien brushed at the fur on its face and made the sound again. Kyreol stared at it uncomprehendingly. Then she said, "Oh." Water was falling out of her eyes. "Tears," she said. "Tears. I had a dream. It made me sad." She brushed away the last of them. *Maybe*, she thought hopefully, *I was just remembering the dead from the spaceship* . . .

Joss Tappan.

She leaned back against the wall, pulling her thoughts together.

I have to find out what happened to Joss.

I have to contact the Dome.

I have to . . .

The alien was rising.

It seemed even more formidable than Kyreol remembered, huge and brilliant with color. Its eyes were a deep purple; it was unafraid at the moment. It walked to the center of the room; its beak clicked

71

at Kyreol. Kyreol stood up after a moment and bundled the raincoat back into her pack. There wasn't much to be done sitting in a dust-covered room. She slung her pack over her shoulder. The alien had turned and was already at the bubble-door.

When it walked fast, Kyreol had to jog to keep up with it. But its progress generally was by fits and starts. It was, she realized, a shy and fearful explorer. It shied at shadows; it stood worrying at closed doors. Its eyes turned pale at puffs of dust blown up unexpectedly by the wind. It hummed nervously when it crossed rooms full of bulky, inanimate objects of uncertain purpose. But it seemed to move with its own sense of purpose, hesitant and nervous as its passage was. Kyreol followed hopefully. *Maybe its ship is near*, she thought. *Maybe they'll let me signal the Dome. If I can explain* . . . It made noises as it moved, hissing like a pot boiling, clicking, breaking into song, then muttering like some forest animal that had just leaped at its supper and missed. Kyreol, listening, felt a giddiness well up in her. She held it as long as she could, but a series of odd sounds strung together— parrots squawking, a blast like a boat horn, more mutterings, followed by a yelp as a little ghost of dust whispered across its path—made her stop suddenly, lean against a wall, crying and trembling helplessly with laughter.

The alien's shadow fell over her. It came so close she could smell it: a faint, sharp odor, like charred wood. She tried to quiet herself, hiccupping, half-alarmed. When she glanced up; all three eyes had turned green.

She sank down in the passageway, whimpering again, half with laughter, half with fear. The green eyes gazed at her; the alien was oddly quiet. What did the green mean? Was it angry? She covered her face with her hands, trying to escape from everything at once: the alien, the lifeless city, the dead spaceship, the unknown moon, the dream of death.

Terje, she whispered, deep inside her.

She smelled the alien again. It had settled beside her. She could hear, faint as breathing, the high, sweet voices of its young.

She lifted her head slowly. The alien was holding something in front of her: a small white and purple furball with a soft beak. Its tiny eyes were closed. It sang as it nuzzled between the three rough fingers, nibbling at them delicately. The alien's eyes, watching it, were still green.

Kyreol sat still. She didn't dare touch the youngling, though its fur looked soft as forest moss, and it might have sung in her hands. It was a soothing thing to look at. Even the alien was calmed by it; the noises it made were gentle and melodious. It put the youngling back finally onto its shoulder, where it nestled into deep fur. Slowly the color of its eyes changed back to purple.

Green, Kyreol decided finally, was its maternal color. The mother worrying over an alien afflicted by a sudden, acute attack of bizarre or distressed behavior. The mother shutting out the world, playing with her young.

But was it female? Kyreol, eyeing it as it searched through the instruments at its kneebands, recognized no evidence one way or another. *Maybe*, she thought, *it's babysitting*.

It found what it wanted among its instruments: a slim silver square with a couple of lights on it. It touched one of the lights and Kyreol, recognizing it, held her breath. It was a communicator. The alien clicked at it, listened. It touched the light again and again. But the only answer was the sigh and rattle of wind through the city.

The alien gave up finally, making a noise like a broken spring. It held the instrument out to Kyreol, and she remembered the com-crystal in her pack. She rummaged for it. It flashed in her hand, gathering light like a star; the alien muttered nervously. Then it reached out, touched the hard, clear crystal curiously. Kyreol opened it, and the alien murmured again at the filigree of gold and crystal within.

"Joss," Kyreol said to the dead world beyond the city. "Joss Tappan. It's me, Kyreol. Are you alive? Joss?"

She didn't know how long she spoke. A rough, three-fingered hand closed around her hand and the com-crystal, stopping her. She sat in silence, her throat raw, the tears aching around her eyes. She didn't want to look at what sat beside her. It didn't know her world, it couldn't speak her name. A youngling hummed in her ear. The alien itself was so still it drew Kyreol's eyes finally. She turned her head slowly, reluctantly, found all its eyes closed. It sat limply, not even fondling its young.

Kyreol stared. *It's lost too*, she thought. *Just like me*.

Its ship doesn't answer; no one answers me. I wonder —I wonder—

"Is that what happened?" she breathed. "Did we hit each other—your ship and mine?"

One eye opened at her voice. It was very pale, almost white. A small sound came finally in response. The other eyes opened. And gradually color returned. The creature gave a very human sigh and got to its feet again.

Kyreol trailed it through a maze of corridors, open walkways, empty rooms, which might have been warehouses or meeting chambers or even marketplaces. There was no one to say what they had been. They kept to the uppermost level of the city, sometimes walking in wind and light, sometimes within the endless, colorless stones. *Maybe it's looking for a door out*, Kyreol thought puzzledly, sweating to keep up with its long, erratic strides. Then the alien, stepping through a door, stopped so suddenly she bumped into it and felt, for the first time, the softness of its fur.

She stepped aside, peering around it, and saw a vast, circular chamber with a clear domed roof. Its two sections were almost completely drawn open to the sky. In the center of the huge room, like a squat glittering insect with a broken wing, sat a very dusty shuttle.

The alien and Kyreol made the same noise. The alien moved cautiously, peering all around. Kyreol ran toward the shuttle, coughing at the dust she kicked up. Its broken wing was a ramp that had never been pulled away. Kyreol went up. The shuttle's wide, round door was open. Its instrument panel was buried under dust.

Kyreol brushed at it, more out of curiosity than hope. How many years had it sat there in the deserted city? Where had everyone gone, leaving the last, unnecessary shuttle? They had flown away; no one had stayed to close the dock roof. Why? She gazed out the roof, at the sky, so full of light and dust it was almost as pale as the moon. "Where did they go?" she wondered, seized with longing to know the story behind the dead city. How many people had been there? Had they had children, cooking pots, carpets, pets, teapots, chairs—had they moved everything? Or was it all still there, beneath them, in a different level of the city? Were there deserted rooms with beds and clothes and little treasures and good-luck charms still in them?

She had a sudden, fleeting memory of Arin Thrase's museum, with her mother's feather betrothal skirt hanging within a glass case.

She drew her eyes back to the instrument panel. The dust poured into her lap, around her feet. Even if she unburied it, it would never fly; its mechanisms were probably clogged. And what had they used for fuel? She scraped clear a circular instrument face, with a desultory movement. Radar? Fuel gauge? A radio? It could have been anything, for all the colored lines across the circle made any sense—

She blinked, hunching over it. Blue. Yellow. Lavender. Pink. Orange. Purple. Brown.

Colors. The first colors she had seen in the entire city.

She stared at the minute patterns of colored lines until they swarmed together under her nose. Then she sat back in the long ample chair realizing she couldn't possibly imagine any kind of people who used color only in tiny symbols on the instrument panels of their ships.

"It doesn't make sense," she murmured. "Unless they just don't care for colors. They just use them for markers."

Then she looked toward the alien.

It stood with its back to her, doing some dusting of its own along a shelf at the far side of the room. Kyreol squinted through the haze on the shuttle's window. "Kyreol, you turtle-brain—" she said aloud. Instead of rushing to a shuttle craft that was choked with dust and full of mysteries, the alien had found other things a landing dock might hold. Flight screens to watch incoming vessels. Computer terminals. A communications system far stronger, if it still worked, than her com-crystal.

She swung out of the shuttle, down the ramp. Sweat pricked at her hairline, brought on by both fear and hope. If it worked, if it was strong enough . . . They could put out a distress signal to the Dome ships. If the alien could make it work . . . the alien turned as she neared it. Its eyes were almost black with excitement; its beak clicked so fast she wondered how anyone could possibly keep track of such a language. She helped it dust, and saw, with a deep surge of hope, that the controls were all encased in clear protective covers.

They worked down the length of the long, curved shelf, dusting, removing covers, removing the fine, fine blanket of dust that had crept even beneath the tightly fitting covers. And all along the control shelf, Kyreol saw again and again the tiny patterns of colored lines.

The number of lines and their positions changed constantly; there might be two lines paralleling, or as many as ten radiating outward from a point. The colors seemed to vary as arbitrarily. The colors themselves were amazingly diverse.

Did they go look at a forest, Kyreol wondered, *to know all those shades of green?* Or did they just invent them, the way we invented—

Numbers. Letters. That's what she was looking at. Instructions, code letters, words as simple as "on" and "off," in an alphabet of color.

She made a sound of wonder and despair, staring at the huge panel. It would take a hundred years to translate color into language—especially when the language itself was of another world. But the alien didn't seem dismayed. It was humming gently, surveying the board, its eyes still the deep, lustrous purple-black. *It understands these things*, Kyreol thought. *Its people don't fly between planets, they fly between stars. They must have met other aliens, recognized many kinds of languages . . .*

The alien stretched a finger toward the panel, moved a switch.

A thousand lights blazed along the panel, halfway up the wall. Kyreol caught her breath and shouted, "You made it work!"

The alien yipped, startled. Its children sang.

9

TERJE SAT on a rock in the dark, watching moon-light shiver into fragments across the water. It was very late; the Healer had been asleep for hours. The moon was beginning to set behind the Face. Regny hadn't returned from the Outstation yet. If he didn't come soon, Terje thought, the moon would disappear and they would miss each other in the dark.

The moon. His eyes were dragged to it. Its light seemed to melt against the black line of cliff as it sank, turning the Falls a milky white. He saw the Moon-Flash in his mind, the lick of fire that had awed him as a child. It made the Healer's dream seem even more perplexing.

"How?" he wondered aloud to the murmuring River, "can I chant to a supply ship?"

He stirred restlessly, wishing Regny would come. Regny would expect him to be asleep; he wasn't sleepy. He was wide awake, his veins full of night, his brain running like a squirrel with unanswered questions. Kyreol. The Healer's dream. What he,

Terje, was going to do. Dreams. Were they sometimes more hope than truth? How much longer would the Healer live? How much did Nara know of what had happened to Kyreol? Where was Regny?

He picked a broken seedpod out of a crevice in the rock and plopped it in the water. A hand came down on his shoulder.

His skin jumped. "Regny—"

"I am so tired," Regny said. "I wish I could turn into something else." His voice sounded heavy, ragged, though his breathing was steady. "What are you doing awake? Is the Healer— Did he—"

"He's sleeping," Terje said. The last glowing bit of moon sank; Regny's face became little more than a solid patch of darkness. He tried to see it anyway. "Did you talk to Nara?"

"Yes."

"Well, what?" Terje said, numbed by his silence. "What did she say?"

"The ship to Xtal never made it. But—" He was gripping Terje's wrist, talking quickly, and Terje realized slowly that he himself had moved, had spoken. He was halfway down the rock. "Whatever happened, happened fast, but they managed to send a distress signal just before they vanished. I told Nara about the Healer's dreams of Kyreol. She cried. She said if the Healer dreamed Kyreol was alive, she is alive. She said perhaps the ship crashed on one of Niade's moons; the signal was so brief no one could tell for sure, but they were in that area. The Dome had been thinking the ship might have destructed in flight, or fallen toward Niade and burned itself up in

81

the atmosphere. Even so, they sent out a couple of search and rescue ships, but they weren't sure where to look. Now they've got something to go on—" He had let go of Terje's wrist; his hand was between Terje's shoulders. It was a long time before Terje could speak. The River blurred and blurred again under his eyes; his fingers were trying to knead implacable stone.

"She's all right," Regny said gently. "She must be. The Healer said so."

"Dreams."

"His dreams are true. You know that. Even I know." He paused as if wondering why Terje took no comfort in that. "He was the one who knew she was in trouble in the first place."

"Regny—"

"She had a bad feeling about the trip—they both did, I think, Nara and Kyreol, but—"

"She said she would see me again. She said that." He slid off the rock, sat on the bank with his back against it, his head tilted back, his eyes closed. He wiped at his face with the back of his hand, then heard the River's voice again, the River of dreams, the River of the dead. They would have to give the Healer's body to the River; the water would wrap itself around him, bear him on his final journey. His throat burned again.

"Regny—"

"Have you eaten anything? Do you want me to—"

Terje opened his eyes. "Please," he begged. "Please listen to me."

"I thought I was," Regny said bewilderedly. "What's the matter?"

"The Healer had a dream—"

"About Kyreol?"

"No." A predawn breeze stirred across the dark water, carrying cold, familiar smells. "He dreamed about the new Healer."

Regny grunted softly. "He can die in peace, then. That amazes me, how the Riverworld takes care of itself. Who did he dream of?"

"Me."

Regny was so still for a moment he might have vanished in the dark. When he spoke, his voice made almost no sound. "What?"

"That's who he saw. Me." He lifted his head, straining to see Regny's face. His own voice shook. "I don't—I don't know what—I don't feel it—"

"That's crazy. It makes no sense. He's a dying man, catching at a bit of hope. He's delirious—he thinks you're still part of the Riverworld, that you never left—"

"You didn't say he was crazy when he dreamed Kyreol was in trouble. He was absolutely right. Regny, I'm scared. Can I say no to a dream? Do I even have a choice? Or are his dreams mirrors—mirrors of the future?"

Regny breathed something inaudible. He bent down next to Terje, pulled something out of his boot. A light flared between them; they could see each other's faces. Regny's looked as though it had been carved out of the hard black stone of the Face.

"What did he dream?"

"That I—I held the River in one hand and the Moon-Flash in the other. He said it meant the River had chosen me. The Moon-Flash! Regny, how can I—"

"You can't. If that's not what you want. You'd have to want it. In your heart. Wouldn't you?"

Terje felt himself relax a little. "I would think so. That's what frightened me. That he saw something I couldn't see, but that his seeing would make it true anyway. There's never been a Healer in my family. Kyreol was always the one with all the good dreams . . ."

"I still think," Regny said softly, "he just invented some hope for himself, so that he could die without feeling he failed the Riverworld."

"Maybe. But his mind seemed clear. He said he knew you."

"What?"

"I mentioned you—that you'd helped me and Kyreol go downriver. No more than that. But he recognized you when I said your name. He said he saw you many times at rituals. He thought you were a ghost, wandering in and out of the Riverworld. You looked like a hunter, but your mind—your thoughts were different."

He heard Regny swallow. Regny was silent; they both were. A bird cried softly, once. Terje touched his eyes again, felt the tears slide under his fingers.

"It's too much," Regny whispered. "It's too much. Do you want to return to the Dome?"

"I can't leave him. Korre's mother said—she said— a day or two at the most."

"Then you go back. I'll stay for the rituals. You can't worry about both the Healer and Kyreol."

"He knows all the rituals. The burial ritual. The ritual for the new Healer. There's no one to perform them."

"That's not your concern," Regny said. "You don't know them either."

"No." He leaned back, his face quieter. "I don't know what to say to him when he wakes and looks at me. There's no time to teach me anything, anyway. He's too sick."

"Then don't worry about it."

"I do worry. When he's gone, what will become of the Riverworld without a Healer?"

Regny was silent again. He ran his hand through his hair, sighing. "I don't know. I do know that all this shouldn't have fallen on your shoulders."

Terje shrugged slightly, as if settling a burden. Regny rose, giving him a quick pat on the way up.

"Come on. Let's go downriver where we can build a fire. You need sleep, and I'm starving."

TERJE WOKE at noon the next day. He lay without thinking, watched the green leaves overhead tremble against the blue sky. They sifted the light, loosed it in patches of gold on the sand. He remembered, briefly and intensely, waking with Kyreol beside him on the River, farther down. The air had been that warm, laden with gold. Kyreol had leaned over, out of her dreams, and kissed him, betrothed as she was to Korre, and he had known then that she would never return to the Riverworld.

Kyreol.

The Healer.

He turned his head, saw the River.

He got up, sighing, brushed the sand and leaves off his face, and walked straight into the water until it rose above his head and he floated on it, letting it carry him like a twig until he was finally awake. Then he waded out, ate a handful of nuts, and walked back upriver to the Healer's house.

He sat at the Healer's side, drinking tea, waiting for the Healer to speak of his dream again. But Icrane's mind was roaming earlier years, when Nara was with him and a tiny Kyreol brought him shells and flowers and small stones, chattering like a bird.

He said abruptly, interrupting his own memories, "I sent them dreams, so they won't grieve."

Terje put his cup down carefully, feeling a cold finger of wonder down his spine. "How can you know?" he whispered. "Can you be sure they'll dream your dreams?"

The Healer smiled. His face was grey-black, sunken, slick with sweat, but his eyes were peaceful. "Everything is one. We are as close as dreams, always. You know that."

"I don't dream like you do. I have simple dreams."

"Kyreol was always with you."

"What—"

"She dreamed for you."

"She—" He paused, blinking, groping at the Healer's meaning. "She won't stay with me here," he said finally.

Icrane only said tranquilly, "I know."

Terje felt something deep in him grow hard and crystal-clear, focusing his thoughts. *I won't leave her. Not for this. Not for anything.* He didn't speak, but Icrane saw the change in his eyes. His smile only deepened a little, as if he were pleased.

"The world," he said, his voice so fragile each word sounded new, "dreams, and the dream is the World. You will know—all that you need to know."

The hardness in Terje snapped. He leaned forward, his face against the pallet, felt the Healer touch him. "I don't," he pleaded. "I don't know anything. I don't know herbs or teas, or what happens in the betrothal caves. I don't know the words to any ritual. Dream again. The Riverworld must have a Healer. I'm not a healer. I belong to the Dome. Dream someone else. I'm ignorant; I don't have any gifts; I don't dream the future—I'm not the one the Riverworld needs. Dream again. Please."

"I did," Icrane said. He smoothed Terje's hair affectionately. His voice came from very far away, from another dream, another place. "Don't be afraid. Everything is simple. Look—" His hand slid down next to Terje's cheek. "Look," he whispered. Terje raised his head.

He moved a moment. His bones were stiff, as if he had been kneeling at Icrane's side for hours. The trembling began as he rose. Korre's mother, stirring soup, dropped the spoon in the pot with a clatter.

She moved swiftly, bent over the Healer's body. Terje stepped away, went to the open door. He felt, gazing at the sunlit River, the young men fishing, the women washing clothes, as if he were a stranger not only to the Riverworld, but to the entire planet. There must be, he sensed, a special burial ritual for a Healer. But what it might be, he had no idea. All ritual, he realized slowly, had died with Icrane.

A sound broke out of him, of sorrow and terror. *Now what?* he thought, his heart pounding. *Now what?* A woman bent over her washing at the far side of the river stopped moving. She stared across at him, sensing something. She touched the woman beside her, pointed.

There was a hiss inside the house. Terje coughed on a sudden wave of smoke. Korre's mother had put the fire out. The women across the water rose slowly, wet clothes in their hands.

And then, as he looked back at them, helpless, afraid, and lonely, the world straightened itself out under his eyes. *Everything is simple*, Icrane had said. *Look.* He was still Terje of the Dome and of the Riverworld. He stood on familiar earth, watching the River he had been born beside. He knew no ritual words, but he knew what was in his heart. The future—any future—was simply one step at a time out of the heart.

He sagged against the doorway, feeling the tears on his face. Icrane himself had seen the world beyond the Falls, had summoned change into the Riverworld. Terje was part of the change, and somehow the dream of Terje had brought peace to the Healer.

Regny was walking up the river toward him. But Terje lingered in the doorway, death at his back, the life of the Riverworld in front of him, knowing, without knowing how he knew, that every step he took now would be a step into the Healer's final dream.

10

NIGHT HAD seeped again into the white city, and the alien and the computer were still talking. Kyreol sat in a corner and watched. Now and then a screen would light up, show a graph or a sweep of stars or an image from Niade's watery surface. The alien would make noises at it, and the screen would darken.

Kyreol's eyes closed, opened again. She had eaten something dry from her pack. The alien did not seem interested in food. Its children were sleeping, little motionless bumps of color in its neck fur. Kyreol wondered at them ceaselessly, fascinated. They were so tiny, compared to the seven-foot alien. They seemed to need nothing except what they found burrowing into the thick fur. Did they drop off like seedpods when they grew too big to be carried? And after, did they still cling to their parent, like human children, needing to be given food, shelter, knowledge, understanding? Or did they become self-sufficient very fast? She imagined a swarm of fur-puffs with legs, all coming up to the alien's knee, making demands in their high voices, practicing all the noises they knew. How many were there? Once she had counted six. Another time ten. Ten children, all growing up at once. Did the alien have to raise all of them all by itself?

Her eyes closed again. She tugged the raincoat closer, chilly in the moon's night. She didn't want to sleep, she wanted to watch the screens. But her eyes kept falling . . . She let them stay closed for just a moment . . .

She saw her father's face. He was smiling at her, peacefully. His lips moved; he seemed to say her name.

Kyreol.

She opened her eyes, stared into the shadows. Her throat made a small, scratchy sound. What was that? A dream? But she hadn't been asleep . . . And why Icrane's face here, on a moon far removed from the Riverworld?

She remembered then the dark, harsh, sorrowing face Terje had held in his hand in her last dream. She made another noise, shaking her head. The alien turned to gaze at her.

It wasn't possible. It couldn't be possible. Icrane's face had been so calm, as if he were handing her a cup of morning tea. But what was Terje doing in her other dream, with the River in his hand and the Moon-Flash on his forehead?

What was going on in the Riverworld?

She pushed the blanket aside restlessly and stood up, went to the alien's side. Its big hands moved across colored lights and clusters of symbols. The image on a screen shifted, turned white. Kyreol watched it a moment, then sighed. It was just the moon's surface, on the day side, with one of its interminable dust storms. The image changed. More dust storm.

The alien made a sound like a shrieking tea kettle. It patted Kyreol on the back and pointed to the screen. Kyreol blinked, her mind working very slowly.

Images of the moon . . . on the day side . . .

How?

Cameras, somewhere. Or some kind of information-gathering equipment.

So?

She shook her head slightly, her breathing quickening. The image changed again, this time to a line of twilight melting into black. "We can see," she whispered. "If they're out there—Joss or your people—we can see them—" She moved closer to the screen, staring at it, waiting for the next change of image to bring her Joss's face. The alien made a small pop, like a mud bubble breaking, and went back to work.

It terrified itself once, miscalculating. The great dock gate overhead began to grind closed with a noise like a building collapsing. The alien sat down on the floor, wailing; all its eyes disappeared and its hands covered the younglings. Kyreol, alarmed, touched a light at random. The computer wailed, too, an astringent, ear-splitting complaint at misuse.

"I'm sorry!" Kyreol shouted at it, her hands over her ears. The alien's head went down between its knees at the racket.

But somehow, eventually the alien found courage enough to uncurl itself and sort out the problems. It pointed at the screen again, and Kyreol settled down to watch, scarcely breathing, lest she miss small figures fighting through the dust.

After half an hour, her eyes were heavy; she could scarcely hold them open.

Dust.

Dust.

More dust.

Why, she wondered, breathing deeply, pulling herself straight, would people put cameras all over such a wasteland? Unless they were just seeing the same patch of land again and again. The images were coded; their coordinates were marked; but what two blues and four yellows and forty-eight other different colors meant, she had no idea.

For shuttles, maybe? To watch their flight across the surface?

Another screen, above the first one, blinked awake. Niade. Its moons, in varying stages of light and dark, arranged with eerie beauty around the planet. The stars.

Thanos.

She jumped when she saw it. It filled the screen; she recognized the green and brown swirls of land beneath the clouds. And there was the river—her River, crawling down half the world, parting the deserts to reach the sea.

Home.

She pointed at it, turning to the alien. Its beak clicked unintelligibly. Its fingers skimmed across the panel of lights and buttons. A sound came out of the panel, a warning. Then a beam of color streaked out of it, angling upward through the open roof, shooting far out into the night.

Kyreol stared at it. The alien, sinking downward once again in the dust, sang softly.

The signal. Color coming from a colorless moon. The message. *We are here.*

Kyreol looked at the alien. Its eyes were pale again, but the sounds it made seemed content. It stroked the sleeping fur-balls; one eye shut, and then another.

You sleep, Kyreol thought. *You just saved our lives.*

She watched the screen again, marveling at the alien, determined to find its people for it. It was big, ungainly, ugly, loving, nervous, and so intelligent the intricacies of the Dome would probably be child's play to it. She had told it once where her world was; and in spite of all its own fears and troubles, it had remembered . . .

Images changed on the screen every twenty seconds. Dust. Dark. Dust. Dark. Once, she saw her own ship, a mangled silver bird, barely visible in the light of a neighboring moon. Nothing moved . . .

"Joss," she whispered. "Where are you?"

Her thoughts strayed to Terje. What was he doing with the River in his hand? And his face full of sunlight? He was supposed to be in shadows, watching a ritual, so silent within the Riverworld that he disturbed not even a pebble. A sudden, despairing impatience rose up in her. Joss, and Terje, and Icrane . . . What were they all doing, impinging on her dreams, hinting of mysteries, hinting of death? She might as well have been trapped in a vacuum as on that moon, where all her questions were soundless and there was no one to ask.

A tear rolled down her cheek as she watched. She brushed at it with her wrist. I'm just tired, she thought. More dust. Shadows in the dust. She saw Icrane's face again, tranquil, saying her name soundlessly.

The death-statue in Terje's hand.

Terje holding the River.

Her eyes stung. She whispered, "No. Not now. I have to watch . . ." The dust blurred in front of her eyes. "Nothing," she said calmly, "is certain. Nobody can tell me anything yet—no one even knows where I am. There's nothing to be sad about yet . . ." Her voice sank again into a whisper. "Which one? Which of them is the message about?"

The alien stirred behind her. She heard a noise from it. She didn't turn, but instead stared stiffly at the screen, willing herself quiet.

Shadows. Shadows in the wind.

She held out her hand to the alien, gesturing without looking, without knowing if it could understand the gesture.

Something is out there.

It stood behind her, its beak chattering. It touched a light; the image held.

White dust and shadows. The day side of the moon. Dark patches moving against the wind. They were moving closer to the camera, but they weren't getting any clearer. Still dark, smudged beneath streaks of dust. Kyreol blinked, her eyes stinging with tiredness.

They moved so slowly, it seemed; their faces would never become clear.

The alien made a mewing sound. Kyreol stared at the screen, her bones frozen. She tried to blink the image clear, but that's all there was of it: dark, faceless shadows moving across the stormy daylight of the moon. Not human. Not tall, furry aliens. A third kind of people.

She sat down in the dust with a thump. More strangers, another language, more mysteries, more confusions. The alien thumped down beside her. All its eyes closed. Kyreol buried her face against her knees. After a moment, she shifted closer to the bright fur, comforting herself with the warmth and the softness and the random noises of the alien young. The big fingers stroked her hair lightly. The alien made a noise like a sorrowing whale and was still.

11

THE RIVERWORLD people gathered, as night fell, one last time around the Healer's house. Boats, lit by torch fire were poled up the slow currents to cluster in the dark, calm water beyond the house. The hunters came, stepping soundlessly through the forest. The gathering was silent; only very young children spoke now and then, briefly and softly. They all waited. Within the Healer's house, Terje and Regny watched. Icrane's body lay under a blanket of feathers the Riverworld women had sewn for him. A flame burned in an oil lamp. It lit Regny's profile, designs in the various ritual carpets rolled in a corner, a glassy sheen in the dark tumble of feathers over the pallet.

Terje's face was white in the glow, but after so many hours, he was beginning to think again. His cold hands were warming against a clay cup of tea he had chosen, recklessly and at random, from the jars and baskets in the house.

"We have to do something," he said for the sixth

time. Regny nodded. He sipped his own tea and made a face. He put his cup down.

"What is this?"

"I don't know. Regny, Korre's mother has been telling people I'm the new Healer."

"She—"

"She never questioned him. He was the Healer; he made the choice."

"This is getting out of hand."

"We have to do something." He swallowed tea without tasting it. It warmed him unexpectedly; the blood flowed back into his fingers, his face. His eyes went to the outline beneath the feathers. Regny said nothing, watched him quietly, until the simplest of all thoughts occurred to him.

"We have to bury him."

"That's a good place to start," Regny said gently. "How?"

"In the River. Everyone is buried in the River."

"Even the Healer?"

Terje looked at him without seeing him, trying to think as the Riverworld might think, of special places, places of mystery and honor. "The Face," he whispered. "The Falls . . . I wonder if there's a secret ritual place behind the Falls. Regny—" He paused, on the edge of some decision. Regny waited. "Regny—"

"I'm listening."

"The Dome would know. The Agency. They've been studying Riverworld ritual for centuries."

Regny opened his mouth, closed it. "You want to bring the Agency into this?" he asked incredulously.

Terje nodded. His face was losing its frozen, dazed expression, growing calm again, as he contemplated the problem.

"There's no other choice," he said. "Is there? I could just tell the people the Healer was wrong, I can't take his place. But he still must be buried. He must be given back to the River. Everyone would feel better if it's done the way it should be. I'd feel better."

Regny drew breath. "So would I," he admitted. "He deserves that."

"Yes."

"Do you want me to go back to the Outstation?"

"Can't you call from here?"

"I can't talk to Nara from here, not with a com-crystal. It won't carry to the Dome. But I'll call the Outstation, have them relay the message, and the information. That still might take a while." He added, "I don't know what the Agency will think."

"It's best for the Riverworld."

"I know that. And you know. But—"

"They'll do it," Terje said. "Because they'll have no choice. Do you know what I think, Regny? I think Nara should come back for this. Tell her."

"How do you think she'll feel?" Regny asked quietly. "Returning, after all these years, just to see him buried?"

Terje's eyes strayed again to the great, shadowy wing laid over the Healer. "I came back," he whispered, "for this. Maybe Icrane did know what he was doing. Maybe he was trying to bring the two worlds together finally."

Regny was silent. His eyes narrowed as he looked

at Terje; the hard cast of his expression loosened a little. He said nothing more, just reached down, pulled the crystal out of his boot.

"Orcrow to Outstation Five. Orcrow—"

"Regny," said the outstation beyond the western boundary of the Riverworld. "Outstation Five. What is it? Where are you?"

"In the Riverworld. Don't quote regulations at me, we have an emergency. The Riverworld Healer is dead. We need instructions from the Agency."

"Why don't you just observe—"

"There is no ritual to observe. Yet. There is no Healer."

"What?"

"Just listen. Listen hard. I want you to pass this message on to Nara, at the Cultural Agency."

"But, Regny, what happened to—"

"Shut up. Listen."

Terje went to the door as Regny spoke. The night had deepened. Stars swarmed across the sky; the moon, beginning to rise above the trees, huge, luminous, swallowed starlight in its glow. Ribbons of fire coiled and uncoiled across the dark water. He sensed eyes on him from across the River, from the forest. No one spoke. They simply waited, puzzled perhaps, but trusting the dream and the choice of the dead.

There was a long silence behind him: Regny was waiting, too, for Nara's reply. As he had suspected, it took a long time. Regny rose after a while, brought Terje his cooling tea.

Terje drank it. It made him sweat. His head swam,

and he groped for balance against the door. He swallowed a bitter taste in his throat. The taste brought back a memory; gazing into the empty cup, he gave a soft laugh.

"I should have been more careful . . ." He wiped his forehead and came inside to sit down.

"What was it?" Regny asked tensely.

"Something for a spider bite. I used to get bitten a lot when I was little. I always thought the tea was worse than the bite."

Regny grunted. "It must have worked; you're still alive." The com-crystal made a soft sound; he flicked it open. "Orcrow."

"Outstation Five. I have Nara on another channel. She wants to know why you can't simply follow instructions, proceed according to regulations—"

"What did you tell her?" Regny interrupted. "There are no regulations for this one. One of her agents is solely responsible for the Riverworld ritual, and he doesn't know what to do. We need instructions."

"She wants to know," the Outstation said after a pause, "how you manage to get into these predicaments.

Regny sighed. "I get lucky."

"Do you want me to tell her that?"

"No." He paused. Terje, shivering after the sudden sweat, watched him. Regny ran his hand through his hair—a frustrated gesture belonging to the world of the Dome. Then his eyes focused on the feathery shadow, and his body stilled again with a hunter's stillness. "Tell her this: The Healer, her husband, is dead." There was silence. The crystal spoke again. "Tell her this: Before he died, he dreamed the dream of the new Healer. The new Healer in his dream held the River in one hand and the moon at Moon-Flash in the other." Silence. "Tell her this: The new Healer in the dream was Terje . . . The Healer's choice is known to the Riverworld. Tell her this: The Riverworld is waiting for Terje to bury the Healer. Tell her: All knowledge of the rituals died with Icrane. Ask her: What regulations would she like us to follow?"

There was a long silence. Regny paced a little, then sat beside the cold firebed. Terje, needing something to lean on, settled against the pile of ritual carpets. For a few moments he saw two flames in the oil lamp, two crystals in Regny's hand. He closed his eyes, opened them again. The feathers drew his eyes, dark and restful. His thoughts strayed. He saw Icrane, walking up the edge of the River to the Face, close to the Falls, where he disappeared into some private place to contemplate the Riverworld. His world: life and death, ritual and dream. Sunlight and water, moonlight and forest. Adding a new pattern to the ritual carpets, a new family-sign to a child's face. Births and spider bites, hunters' accidents and misplaced fishhooks. Fire on the dark water and the long list of the dead, the never-forgotten, all the ghosts who, like last year's leaves, added to the rich loam of the world.

Everything is simple.

He opened his eyes. The world was just the world: Riverworld or Dome. The language was different;

the heart of the world was changeless. The River ran to the Dome, connecting; a woman in the Dome remembered in silence the chants she had spoken in the shadow of the Face.

He said again, softly, to Regny, "Tell her to come."

The com-crystal's tone sounded. Regny drew his eyes from Terje. "Orcrow."

"Regny . . ." The voice from the outstation was hesitant. "Nara asks to talk to Terje. Is he with you?"

"Yes." He passed the crystal to Terje.

"I'm here," Terje said.

"She wants to know what you will do. If you have accepted the Healer's dream?"

Terje was silent, groping for words. "The Healer dreamed a dream," he said finally. "I don't know how to say yes or no to it. All I want to do is give him a burial ritual."

"She wants to know: What then? Will you learn to become the Healer? Or will you leave the Riverworld, return to the Dome?"

Terje closed his eyes again, opened them to the shadows. He said patiently, "I don't know. How can I know? It's the Healer's dream, not mine. Ask her to come here."

"What?"

"Ask Nara to come to the Riverworld. Now. Ask her to bring the knowledge of the ritual herself. Please. Ask her to come. She has the right." He paused, trying to hear Nara's answer across the distance.

"She says—"

"Tell her nothing surprised the Healer. He dreamed about the Dome, he dreamed Kyreol's flight between planets, he even recognized Regny. He wanted— Tell her the Dome is just another dream of the Riverworld. Tell her—"

"Wait—"

He waited. Something he said had made Regny smile. The crystal spoke.

"Terje—"

"Tell her," Terje said carefully, insistently, "the Healer said: 'She ate my heart like the moon eats the sun.' He always wanted her to return. His last words were: 'Everything is simple.' Tell her to come."

The crystal was silent. The smile had vanished from Regny's eyes. He leaned forward, drawn like Terje toward the crystal, tense, listening for its voice. But his eyes were on Terje's face, in warning or in wonder.

"She'll be there," the crystal said, "by morning."

12

MORNING. Kyreol stirred, opened her eyes. She was huddled against the alien, using it like a blanket. Its hands were roaming over the playing younglings; it seemed to be waiting patiently for Kyreol to move. She drew away from it; its eyes sought hers, again pale green. She smiled a little, after a moment, wishing she could thank it for permitting her to come so close. The beak clicked softly. She sneezed abruptly, from the cold and the dust; the alien gave a startled hiccup.

They both uncurled stiffly. The alien rose to gaze at the screen. Kyreol went to rummage in her pack for water and something to eat. It turned to regard her curiously as she chewed, its eyes turning the more familiar purple. She wondered what it lived on. Even as she wondered, it reached for something dangling on its knee and turned back to the screen nibbling. She joined it. It held what seemed to be a bar of green and brown seeds it picked at absently with its beak. She showed it her bar of concentrated

proteins and vitamins. It couldn't make a face, but
its sound-slits made a sudden whuff at the smell, and
she laughed.

It gazed at her again. A ghostly echo of her laugh
came out of it. Then it eyed the light signal, diffused
a little in the hot sun pouring through the roof. It
made a noise and turned again to the screen.

Dust.

Light.

Dark.

More light.

More dust.

Kyreol made an impatient, frustrated noise.

A hurricane.

They bumped together, staring at the screen. Dust
whirled wildly in every direction. It began to clog
the equipment, but before the image was blotted out,
a streak of fire splashed across the screen.

Kyreol jumped. The alien reached out instantly,
stilled the image. It went dark. But the coordinates
were still there. Incomprehensible, but there.

"What—" Kyreol breathed. The alien chattered at
her, pointing at the blank screen. It turned her around
finally, its hands on her shoulders, and pointed at
the shuttle.

A ship.

"Someone landed!" She whirled, staring at the
screen. "They saw our light! But where? But where?"

The alien's fingers were racing across the panel
keys. The entire alphabet of color ranged across one
of the other screens. The alien muttered at it awhile,

its eyes the deep, purple-black. Slowly, under its instructions, the tiny lines of color began to break up.

Whose ship, Kyreol wondered, was it? A Dome ship? One of the alien's? Or a ship full of shadows, drawn toward the beacon coming out of the dead city?

I don't care, she thought. *I don't care. I just want to go home.*

Joss. She couldn't go home without Joss. Or the dead within the Dome ship.

"I bet it's close," she said suddenly. The alien, making noises, didn't seem to hear. "If they saw our light, they must have landed as close as possible . . . I bet we could see it if we could just look out the right window. If we could find a window."

Her eyes strayed over the dock.

Or climb on the roof.

The bubble-people didn't seem to care for ladders. And the dock itself, shielded against the dust, looked only upward.

How, she wondered, while the alien was busy with its mysterious computations, *can I get on the roof?*

If she could fly the shuttle . . . But even if she could—an extremely remote possibility—she'd have to rise near the message light. And there was no telling what kind of damage that might do if she wasn't careful.

Besides, it would upset the alien, and she owed it too much to upset it now.

She sighed, feeling useless. The alien made a garbled noise. Hope? Frustration? Success? She had a sudden vision of its planet, full of beings all muttering a constant, complex string of peculiar sounds as they went about their daily business. How did they ever sort out all the sounds? Did they say simple things with their beaks, like "Good morning?" Or did they just blat at one another, like mud-holes conversing?

"Kyreol."

Her skin prickled with shock.

"Kyreol."

A voice from the console.

The alien backed away from it with a whistle of surprise. Kyreol sprang toward it.

"I'm here!" she cried. "I'm here! It's me, Kyreol. Me." She pointed at herself. "Kyreol."

The alien gave another whistle. Then it matched sounds out of its vast, unpredictable repertoire.

"Kyreol," it said hollowly. Its hands shifted across the panel, hovered, then touched a light.

"Kyreol."

"I'm here," she said to the light. She leaned over it, weak with relief. "I'm here . . ."

"Are you all right? This is Wayfarer, from the Dome. We've been searching for you. Are you all right? Where are you?"

"I'm in the city. Can you see it?"

"Affirmative. We landed almost on top of it."

"Can you see the green light?"

"Yes! It led us here. How— Did you do that?"

"No." She shook her head, half-laughing, half-crying. "No. There's someone with me. Do you want us to come out? What side of the city are you on?"

"We're carrying a small shuttle. Is there room to land through the roof?"

"It's a dock. An empty dock. But the light—"

"We can edge past it. It would be easier to pick you up than for us to try and find each other on foot. Are you hurt at all?"

"No." The laughter in her died suddenly. "No. But —the ship crashed. I'm alive. Joss Tappan—He—I don't know what happened to him. I couldn't find him anywhere. The others are dead." She added, at the silence. "I covered them against the dust. We have to bring them home."

"Yes. Don't worry. We'll be with you in a few moments."

"Don't scare the alien. It's very shy."

The voice from Wayfarer rose. "Kyreol! There are no aliens on this moon!"

"There are now. Please," she said anxiously, "hurry."

She look at the alien, missed it, then looked down. It was sitting on the floor under the panel, its eyes pale pink, as nervous as Kyreol would be, anticipating a ship full of its kind. Kyreol gazed at it a moment, uncertainly. Then she sat down beside it, close to the soft fur, the sleeping young, the faint, charcoal smell of its fear. Together they waited for rescue.

The small shuttle eased past the signal light and landed in a whirl of dust. The hatch opened. Kyreol shifted, wanting to run to it. All the alien's eyes were closed; in terror or against the dust, she couldn't tell. Its big shoulders heaved and fell in a breath. One eye opened. It looked at her palely. Then, very slowly, it got up, tugging at her until she rose.

"Kyreol," it said, and pointed to the shuttle crew, in flightsuits and helmets, leaping to the floor.

She ran.

They tried to hug her, take their helmets off and talk all at the same time. She knew them: Miko Ko, a woman from the Interplanetary Agency, one of Joss Tappan's coworkers, and a young, light-eyed man, Cay Tappan, Joss Tappan's nephew, one of the Inter-systems pilots.

"Nara will be glad to see you," Miko Ko said huskily, stroking Kyreol's dusty hair. Cay Tappan was staring across the room at seven feet of fur.

"Who is that?"

"Don't scare it," Kyreol pleaded.

"It's scaring me. I've been all over this system and I've never seen anything—anyone like that." He took in the flashing lights and lit screens behind the alien. "You got all this working? This place has been dead for fifty years."

"The alien did. It saved us. I didn't do anything; it did everything. I think it crashed at the same time we did. It's from another star system."

Cay Tappan whistled. The alien, rocking a little on its feet, opened one eye at the sound.

"It likes soft noises," Kyreol said. "It has three eyes. It's scared now, but at least it opened one. It has babies."

"What?"

"On its shoulders. They're very tiny. They sing." She paused, feeling as if she were telling one of her childhood stories. Miko Ko's mouth was open. "If you sing to it, it likes that."

"Well," Miko said in a rush of breath, with all the Agency's readiness for good-will among neighbors. "Whatever it likes."

She hummed a few tones. The alien's other eyes opened.

They sang to each other for a while. Soon, they were standing together at the console panel, pointing, gesturing, inventing a language as they went along, of stray noises and body movements. The alien showed them, with its star map, where it had come from. Then it activated the scanning screen again, and they watched silently the monotonous patterns of storm and darkness around them.

"Joss is out there somewhere . . ."

"How do you know?" Cay asked gently.

"He wasn't on the ship. I looked everywhere. He wasn't there." She paused. "Also—there's someone else out there. A sort of bulky, faceless, shadowy people, walking in the wind. They scared both of us. We saw them on the screen."

Cay stared at her. "Are you sure?"

"We saw them."

"It's a small, very barren moon," Miko objected. "Nothing lives here."

"I'd better check it out . . ." He eyed Kyreol. "Do you want to go to the ship?"

She shook her head. "I want to come with you. I want to find Joss. But I don't want to leave the alien alone."

"I'll stay with it," Miko said. She smiled as they

stared at her. "I like it. I'm good with languages. Maybe we can find a way to talk. Or click. Or something."

Kyreol touched the alien to get its attention. She pointed to herself and Cay, then to Wayfarer's shuttle, and finally tapped the scanning screen a few times, until the alien, standing stock-still, made a huff of comprehension. It stroked its young, its eyes paling, then darkening as it stroked Kyreol's hair, as if she were one more of its younglings, and clicked at her briefly.

"I'm staying," Miko said. "Miko."

It gave a sudden, startling imitation of Kyreol's laughter.

KYREOL, strapped in the shuttle, watched the white city fall away from them as they rose. Cay Tappan was busy staying away from the light beam, but she hung over her seat, staring down, seeing the empty patterns of domes, and stairs and tiered walls with their walkways leading to the abandoned room.

"What was it?" she whispered. "Whose was it?"

"It was an experiment. The people of Niade built it—the strongest, the most courageous of them. It was to be part factory, part space station for its explorers, part laboratory. It had room for generations of families. They must have stayed for—maybe twenty years. Then, even the most ambitious of them gave it up."

"Why?"

"To return to Niade. To return to the seas. They

were dying away from their home planet. They were like fish trying to live on a desert. Theoretically, their bodies could stand it. They thought succeeding generations would wean themselves away from the seas. But the tides were in their blood—literally. The sea pulled them back."

"It's not easy to leave your home."

"You'd know that."

"It was easier for me. But the alien . . . To be that fearful, and yet to leave its home to explore—it's braver than anyone I've ever met. Except," she added, "my mother. The alien had its ship. I had Terje. My mother just had her betrothal feathers."

Cay smiled. He explained to Wayfarer, which stood like a very tall, very slender mushroom beside the city, what they were doing. The little shuttle picked up speed as it left the city. It skimmed across the blustery surface, heading in the general direction of the crash. So close to the ground, the billowing, feathery dust made it difficult to see. Kyreol kept blinking, trying to clear her eyes, when it was the dust beyond that was blurring her vision. In such a shifting landscape, she realized, anything might form . . . a few dark stones might turn into shadows walking against the wind.

Did we see them? she wondered. *Didn't we?*

The ship appeared under them suddenly, a broken, silvery husk half-covered already with dust. Cay made a soft sound. He landed close to it.

"Stay here," he said briefly, and Kyreol nodded gratefully.

He was gone a long time. Panic overtook her,

building slowly out of the loneliness, the constant whip and chatter of dust, no horizon to see, no sky— and the ship itself, gashed and twisted metal, the dead within already being slowly buried. Staring at it, she realized how close she had come to death.

She put her hands over her mouth, reliving the terror, grieving once again. Cay, opening the hatch, made her jump.

"Don't cry." His own eyes were red-rimmed in his dusty face. He put his arms around her. "Kyreol, I don't know how you survived that. And then to find shelter for yourself, to find help from the most unlikely looking source— You've done well."

"Joss?" she asked, wiping her eyes on her sleeve. He started the shuttle again.

"You were right. I couldn't find a trace of him. We'll come back for the dead later."

They found the encroaching line of twilight and skimmed through it. Cay spoke again to Wayfarer, giving them the coordinates of the crashed ship. Then he spoke to Miko; she had seen nothing new on the screens. Kyreol stared out at the distant night. The storm abated after an hour or so; the dust began to settle. The storm had concealed nothing. The surface was powdery as far as the eye could see. Not a rock on it, black or white. Nothing even to cast a shadow. Cay angled out of the twilight, sped across the sunlight again.

Shadows.

She straightened in her seat. They were long, lean, stroked across the surface by the setting sun. Four of them. Shadows far out of proportion to the figures who cast them, moving slowly across the fading daylight, still hunched against the dust as though, after fighting it for hours, they hadn't realized the storm was over.

She made a sound. Cay turned his head quickly. Big, darkly fluttering, faceless . . . One of the shadows divided, separating into itself and a smaller fifth shadow, which, feeling the still air, lifted a dark cover and revealed a face to the setting sun.

"Joss!"

13

NARA RETURNED to the Riverworld with the sun. Regny had made yet another journey to the Outstation to meet her as she landed and to escort her through the forests. Terje stayed in the house with the Healer's body. It shouldn't be left alone, he felt; that was a mark of respect. He felt also, dimly, that if he stayed close to it, perhaps something of the thoughts and dreams that had filled the house might wander into his head and help him make sense of the Healer's wishes. But his thoughts remained familiar: he was just Terje, even-tempered and full of good will, but with no more foresight than a bird.

Worn out, he fell asleep beside the still figure under the dark cloud of feathers. Even in his sleep, he found himself talking to the Healer, explaining why nothing had been prepared yet for the burial.

Nara's coming, he said. *She'll know what to do. You see, I don't know what to do, I don't know anything.*

You left without telling me anything. But when she comes, everything will be done as it should be.

It will be good to see her again, the Healer said peacefully. *Tell her I said that*. His voice seemed to come from two places: from beneath the shadow of feathers and from beside Terje, just out of eyesight, as if the Healer sat once more at his own firebed, sipping tea while Terje slept.

I will, Terje promised.

You see, the Healer said. *Nothing was really lost, was it? The world dreams itself. The rituals are preserved. They aren't lost; they're simply in a different place within the dream.*

But how can I chant to the Moon? Terje pleaded. *Make me understand that. The Moon-Flash is just—*

The Moon-Flash. There was a soft sound, as if a teacup had been placed on the ground. *Why are you so afraid? What have I said to make you so afraid?*

I can't become you, Terje said to the dark. *I know too much, and I don't know enough. I can't dream for anyone—*

You love the Riverworld, Icrane said simply. *That's enough for the Riverworld.*

But—

Now you sound like Kyreol.

Kyreol. She won't come here. I won't leave her.

Terje, the Healer said gently. *Stop worrying. Here. Drink this tea. You'll feel better.*

He stretched out his hand, not toward the firebed, but toward the motionless feathers. *Dream*, the Healer said from beneath them. *Dream* . . . The feathers swirled over his eyes, settled over him, covered him with their airy darkness. *I'm dead*, he thought. Then: *No, I'm Icrane.*

I'm Terje.

I'm a bird.

Flying between the River and the Moon, he saw the simple silver curve of water away from the Face that was the Riverworld. He felt such a confusion of love and fear for it that he reached down, picked the River up, held it protectively. The water flowed in and out of his grasp; he felt its endless life and strength. With his other hand, he reached toward the full moon . . .

He woke, blinking. The house was grey with dawn. The world outside was silent, still asleep. He sat up, looked down at his hands as if he expected to find the river still in them.

His lips parted. "They should be there," he whispered. "They should be . . ." He stood up, still half-asleep, enveloped in dreams, and soft feathers, not daring yet to think. He searched the Healer's pots until he found his paints.

He had painted the Moon-Flash on one hand and the River on the other, and he was painting his face, using a bowl of water for a mirror, when the light from the rising sun falling in the doorway was blocked and he couldn't see. He looked up.

They stared back at him: Regny in his feathers, Nara in a dark flightsuit. He felt the blood leave his face suddenly beneath the paint. *It's wrong*, he thought at their expressions. *I'm doing it wrong—*

"Terje?" Nara said. Her voice shook. He rose

silently. There were black and white birds on his cheeks and a long stroke of fire across his forehead. Beneath the fire was his sign: Three Rocks. Beneath the signs, his skin was a mask of white paint.

He couldn't speak. She took a step toward him. He held out his palms, half in explanation, half out of a need for confirmation. *I am the Healer*, the signs said, and Nara stopped.

"Terje," she said very softly. "This is correct. I don't—" She stopped to swallow. "I don't understand how you knew. You may have two people to help you: one man, one woman. You sent for me. You do not speak until you begin the ritual chant."

He closed his eyes, felt himself tremble. But the time to think was later, later. When he opened his eyes again, Nara knelt beside Icrane's body, her hand lightly smoothing the feathers, over and over, that covered his hand.

STEP BY STEP, like someone walking an ancient, well-worn path, so familiar underfoot the walker was scarcely aware of it, Terje performed the ritual of the Burial of the Healer.

He finished painting himself, in the silence of the sunlit house. Nara handed him the colors he needed. She didn't speak; the colors spoke for themselves, formed shapes in his mind, which he painted on his face, his wrists, his feet. The entire Riverworld waited patiently beyond the door, trusting him beyond question to know what he was doing. Finally he rinsed his fingers in the water and stood up. Nara set the bowl aside.

He looked down at the hidden figure on the pallet. Nara waited behind him. Regny sat like a statue in a corner, observing, his eyes never leaving Terje's face. The feathers seemed to rustle under Terje's gaze. He lifted his arms suddenly, straight out from his sides, and Nara, beyond questioning herself, gathered the black mantle of feathers up and settled it over Terje's shoulders.

The Healer's body lay exposed, smaller and frailer than Terje remembered. He glanced around quickly, feathers stroking his face. Nara waited until he recognized what he was searching for: the long, worn carpet, plain but for the Healer's sign woven into its center, that the Healer had sat on, year after year, while he explained dreams and brewed his teas.

He bent, but Regny anticipated him. Moving swiftly, urgently, as if he too had become, for a time, completely absorbed into the Riverworld, he lifted the carpet, shook ashes and a scattering of tea leaves out of it, and handed it to Terje, who laid it carefully over Icrane's body, giving it back its privacy.

Terje's shoulders loosened; he sighed softly. For a few moments he stood without moving, an awesome figure in light, wearing a dead-white mask patterned with signs, cloaked from shoulder to sole in black feathers. His mind walked for him: out of the house, up the River, toward the Face. But that was wrong, he sensed. The Healer's body should be in a boat.

A boat poled upriver? But the river current quickened toward the Face, became shallow, furious.

Downriver?

But there was no place of mystery downriver for a Healer to be taken to, except the wide, unnamed mystery beyond Fourteen Falls.

Then he knew. It was, as the Healer had said, simple.

The dead Healer was given back to the River. It was for the new Healer to make the journey, on foot, to the Face.

He turned, looked outside. Icrane's small boat bobbed at its mooring a foot beyond the bank. Things fluttered in it: feathers, late-blooming flowers, small gifts tied and weighted with nuts or shells.

He swallowed a burning in his throat, a looming wonder. They knew . . . as he knew. Looking back into the house, he saw Nara's eyes, wide and glistening with tears. Her expression shook him; he looked away from her quickly, not wanting to become aware of himself.

"The body must be placed in the boat," she said softly to Regny, for Terje had already moved, in his mute certainty, to the head of the pallet.

Regny nodded briefly. His face looked grim, rock-hard, but he moved like a man in a dream, like Terje, not permitting himself to think. They tucked the white carpet around the body, then lifted the pallet. It came up easily; they carried it out into the morning.

The silence, Terje sensed, from the boats had a stunned feel to it; not even a baby cried. Only the wind spoke; the Riverworld people might have been ghosts viewing the face of their new Healer. Then

Nara appeared, another ghost, the Healer's vanished wife, dressed strangely in black, wading into the River to pull the boat close. Terje and Regny laid the covered figure into it gently on its bed of gifts. Then Terje stood still again, his eyes caught by the bareness of the carpet.

Something . . . needed to be there at the Healer's feet.

Something simple.

He went back into the house and the entire Riverworld focused its attention on the empty doorway. He reappeared finally, carrying the Healer's teapot.

Nara's face broke into a smile beneath her tears. Terje laid the pot gently between the Healer's feet. Then he looked at her, waiting. She was the Healer's wife. Her gift would lie on his breast.

She already held it in her hands: the star of the Healer's dream, the voice that had led Kyreol out of the Riverworld. She put it between the hands folded beneath the carpet: the com-crystal, catching light like a tear.

The boats began to separate. Slowly, easing back, away from each other, they were poled toward the opposite bank to form a long, long line that began opposite the Healer's threshold and ended somewhere out of sight. The drifting and maneuvering took time. At last, as the sun crept higher above the trees, the River people passed a stillness up the line from boat to boat. They waited.

Terje, his eyes stinging drily, loosed the mooring line and stepped back.

The River took the boat slowly, little by little,

tugging it lightly away from the bank. It caught on a snag; the water coaxed it free. Its prow swung uncertainly, then steadied. For a long time they watched. A leaf drifted into the boat, clung to the carpet. A bird darted low over it. The River took a firmer hold of it, drew it into midwater, into its slow, deep currents. It began to glide silently past the boats. The strange figure on the shore, the new Healer, masked with signs and mantled in darkness, broke his silence.

The chant was simple: a plea to the River to accept the greatest gift of the Riverworld, its Healer. It was picked up by the people; they spoke it softly, in a wind-murmur, as the boat drifted downriver. It held its course steadily, unwaveringly. Terje had a sudden image of all the Healers from the world's beginning, whose spirits dwelled within the River, reaching up with their hands to guide it. Then he saw Icrane himself, as he had been in life, steering the little boat placidly through the currents, making his own journey into the mysterious world beyond the River.

The vision of Icrane turned into a shaft of sunlight. Terje stirred, no longer able to see anything but the painted stern and the calm parting of water behind it. As he moved, he felt his own body, too warm under the feathers and the stiff, uncomfortable mask of paint on his face.

He knelt down at the River's edge, needing to remove the mask, needing to become Terje again. For a moment he saw himself as Regny and Nara had seen him: a man with a face out of no world they had ever seen or would ever see.

He splashed water over his face quickly, again and

again, until the moon and the fire and the river disappeared, and the last of the white paint washed away. As he stood up, he let the cloak of feathers fall to his feet. The River people still chanted, but they watched him, and he saw the smiles on their faces at him, Terje, who had returned to take his place in the Riverworld.

He drew a quick breath, torn, panicked, and whispered his own plea: "Kyreol."

Then Nara was embracing him, and his fear eased at her touch. He looked at her, dazed, bewildered, while she said huskily, "Terje, thank you. Thank you for bringing me back. For preserving the peace of the Riverworld. For all you did for Icrane in his last hours that I would never have had the courage to do."

"I told him you would be coming. He said—he said to tell you it would be good to see you again."

Her hold slackened; she stared at him. "When?"

He shook his head a little, remembering. "After he died. I'm sorry—I only dreamed it."

She was mute a moment, amazed. Then she took his arm. "Come into the house where we can talk."

"I can't. I can't, yet."

"Ah." She nodded. "I forgot that part. Then her voice dwindled to a whisper. "Terje, how did you know? Who taught you the ritual?"

"Just—it was just there." His eyes went past her to Regny, as if he might hold some key to understanding. But there was only wonder in his eyes.

"The Riverworld," Regny said softly. "Year upon year, century upon century of rituals spoken, woven into the fabric of a small place—trees, the birds, the river itself must know them by now."

"I suppose so," Terje said. He felt his body tugged toward the Face; his mind had already begun to walk the trail toward the Falls, toward some secret place, a Healer's place he would not know until he came to it. "I have to go. Please," he begged them. "Wait for me. Don't leave yet."

"We'll be here," Nara promised, "when you return."

He nodded, mute again, calmed by the promise, and turned away from them to the Face.

14

A FACE CAME into Kyreol's mind. It came out of nowhere, a dream-moment out of the milky, blinding swirl of dust the shuttle disturbed landing. It was painted dead-white, with Riverworld signs on its brow, its cheeks. Its hair was sun-colored; its eyes were dusty-gold. It said, *Kyreol.*

A death mask.

A shudder ran through her, as if all her bones had recognized the mask. Then, abruptly, she was crying, wailing, while Cay, trying to land, stared at her in astonishment.

"Kyreol!"

"I don't know which one of them died! The dreams are so mixed up!" She fumbled for the hatch handle, sobbing.

"Wait—"

"Something's happened in the Riverworld!" The hatch opened finally, just as the shuttle settled; the dust matted her tear-streaked face, and she choked.

The smaller of the dark figures dropped the billowing plastic it had worn as a shield against the wind.

"Kyreol!"

She stumbled out of the shuttle into Joss Tappan's arms.

"It's all right," he said soothingly, shaken. "It's all right—"

She heard a familiar clicking. She turned her head and saw, as the other figures dropped their dark, voluminous shields, four tall aliens with variegated fur and rapidly paling eyes.

The sight made her stop crying for a moment. "Joss," she breathed, "they're—"

"They're very friendly," he said quickly.

"I know."

"What do you mean you know?"

"I know," she said again. "I've been with one. In the dead city. Wayfarer saw the signal—"

"Wayfarer." He straightened then and watched the man emerging from the dust cloud. "Cay!"

Kyreol drew back to look at him. His face was very pale; a purplish, jagged cut down his cheek and jaw was just beginning to close. He smiled as she stared at him anxiously, then said, "I'm all right. I couldn't find you on the ship. I left it to look for you. Kyreol, I can't believe you're alive."

"I was trapped between two airbeds—they broke loose and saved me."

"Are you hurt?"

She shook her head. Then, her face crumpling again, she nodded. "Joss—" She pushed her face against him, hearing a chatter of curious sounds around her. "Someone died in the Riverworld. Either Terje or my father. They keep sending me messages, but I can't— Something happened—"

"Kyreol."

She straightened slowly, wiped her tears, and stood free of him, her face, under its mat of dust, as bizarrely masked as the face in her dream-thought. Joss held her shoulders. She saw the heaviness in his eyes, the hollows of pain in his face.

He said softly, "Please. Just try, for now, to worry about one world at a time."

"Yes," she whispered.

"What city? We've been walking through dust for four days."

"You could see it from the crashed ship. Unless the dust was too thick."

He sighed, his hands loosening. "I wasn't thinking after the crash. I was trying to find you. I wandered into a storm." He looked at Cay again, his bruised face haggard with relief. "How did you find her?"

"They got a signal light going," Cay said, "in the dead city. You remember. The one the people of Niade deserted years ago."

"So that's where we are," he breathed.

"The alien did it," Kyreol said. His attention came back to her.

"I think," he said, "that must be who these people are looking for."

"Yes."

"Will they come into the shuttle?" Cay asked. He

gestured at it, watching them. They seemed less fearful than the alien Kyreol knew, and less noisy. But their eyes were still pale. She turned to them, catching their attention with the movement. She pointed toward the horizon. Then her hands stroked the air above her shoulders very gently and she hummed.

They erupted in a muddle of sounds, their eyes turning purple. Joss asked amazedly under the babble, "What in the world did you say?"

"The one I met carries tiny babies on its shoulders. It hums to them, and they hum back. Joss, it saved our lives. It's from another star-system. It was as scared of me as I was of it. But somehow, we became friends. It figured out the computer system; I showed it where Thanos is, and it sent the signal that Wayfarer saw."

"Miko is with it now," Cay said. Joss was still staring at Kyreol.

"You amaze me," he said simply. The aliens were clustering around the shuttle, making steam-whistle sounds.

"I didn't do anything," Kyreol said surprisedly. "The alien did it all."

Somehow they all managed to fit in the shuttle. It sagged a little, lifting, and refused to fly very high, but in that flat world they could skim the surface without danger. Kyreol, enclosed by fur, smelling the familiar charcoal smell, turned once to search their shoulders. No younglings. One of them, with astonishing courage, touched her hair.

"Did your two ships crash?" Cay asked Joss.

"I think so, but I'm not sure. They weren't with

their ship when I met them. Or rather when they found me lying in the dust. They gave me something to drink; they carry supplies on their kneebands. They put some kind of salve on my face. I don't know what it was, but it felt better. I can't believe," he added, "that people with such a highly sophisticated technology, who can fly between systems, managed to hit our ship."

"Maybe you hit them," Cay suggested.

"There was no reading of another ship. It came out of nowhere. As if—as if it had somehow defied the laws of speed and time. I wish we could talk . . ." He glanced back at Kyreol, disturbed by her silence. Surrounded by four huge, beaked aliens, her face composed, she gave him a small smile. He turned, looking amazed again. Her thoughts slid away from the shuttle, away from the moon, across the river of the night to a tiny, distant world that was sending signals of its own trouble across vast distances with a stunning simplicity.

Terje, holding the River and the Moon, and the statue of death.

Her father, smiling, saying her name.

Terje, his face painted with the River and the Moon-Flash.

The signs of the Healer.

Her lips parted, moved soundlessly. *Terje, what have you done?*

Night was flowing in a dark tide toward the city when they reached it. The aliens' eye colors changed alarmingly. They emitted startled blobs of sound as

Cay, straining the overladen shuttle, managed to bring it high, then ease it down past the guide light into the dock. The shuttle hatches opened to a tangle of fur and flightsuits. At the computer, the alien with the younglings sang a deep, melodious note so loudly that parts of the shuttle vibrated and the humans ducked as if it were a wind blast, covering their ears.

Its eyes turned blue.

The aliens spent a few minutes stroking one another, their beaks clicking furiously. Cay and Joss spoke to Wayfarer, waiting patiently outside, discussing a return to the crash site to pick up valuables, the ship's log and tapes, and the bodies of the dead. Miko was still at the computer. Kyreol went to her side, gazed down at the tiny patterns of color. "Did you figure out their alphabet?"

"I think it's based on a number system," Miko said absently. "One to a hundred . . . A hundred colors, color-patterns repeated with a numerical regularity."

"When I first saw the city, I thought it was built by people who only saw white."

Miko smiled. "It's the moon that has no color. The people of Niade can perceive color-shades indiscernable to most humans. But they took all their possessions, all their colors with them when they went back home."

"They died," Kyreol said softly, "away from their home."

"Yes."

But Terje had never shown signs of wasting away at the Dome. He had loved both worlds: the Riverworld and the Dome. *Or maybe*, Kyreol thought, *it was only me he loved, and I wouldn't leave the Dome. But I would have known if he was unhappy.* She frowned down at the panel, uneasy, disturbed. What had he done, and why? Then she realized what she had been thinking. The frown turned into a knot between her brows; she swallowed hard to keep from crying again.

Icrane.

"I never went back," she whispered drily, "to explain why I had left him."

"Kyreol," Joss said behind her. She turned.

"My father is dead."

His lips parted. "How do you—" He shook his head at his questioning and pulled her to him, held her gently.

"I'm sorry."

"We all left him, and he died without knowing why." Her eyes were still dry, dark as the Face. "But Terje—he's doing something I don't understand. His face is painted like a Healer's. Joss, when we get back—" She drew a deep breath. "When we get back, I'm going to the Riverworld."

"Talk to your mother first. I know you're grieved. But you can't just—"

"I can, too." Then some of the darkness left her eyes. She sighed. "No. You're right. I can't just go running in there like a child, disturbing all the hard work her Agency has done. But I will go as far as I can. I have to see Terje." She clung to him suddenly. "I'm so afraid I've lost both of them."

"No," Joss said comfortingly. "No." But she wasn't comforted.

"Joss, did Wayfarer tell the Dome we're found?"

"Yes. Their reply should come in a few minutes."

"It's so far," she whispered, "between place-name and place-name." She was silent a little, watching the aliens, listening to their noises. "Colors that are letters, sounds instead of smiles or tears . . ."

"Are you sorry you came?"

She thought. Then she drew back, looked at him. "I was afraid I'd travel so far from the Riverworld I would lose it completely from my head. But instead, it just came with me. As long as I can remember in my heart where it is in this mess of stars, I won't be sorry."

He smiled. "Kyreol, you've had a harsher introduction to other forms of highly intelligent life than any one of us ever imagined. Instead of running in fear from someone seven feet tall and covered with fur, you made a friend, you found a way to let it help you. Without that signal, Wayfarer would have searched for weeks. I'm very proud of you."

"I'm glad," she said. But her eyes were troubled again, full of the fragments of dark dreams.

Within the furry, chattering group, the alien with its young turned to look at her.

Its eyes paled slightly, then went slowly green. It came to her, stroked her hair and its busy, humming young, chattering, looking from Kyreol to Joss. Then, in its hollow voice, it said, "Kyreol."

Joss started. "Miko!"

"I'm working," Miko said, "on the clicks."

"You're using an alien system to translate another alien language."

"I know," she said cheerfully. "It's driving me crazy."

"You could draw pictures," Kyreol suggested. "That's what I did. In the dust. Or you could point."

"Primitive," Miko said wryly.

"We want them to come to the Dome," Joss explained to Kyreol. "I suspect their ship is in as bad a shape as ours is. And on the Dome, we have translators. We could learn so much from them. We could provide tools to salvage their ship, perhaps. We could—"

"We could find out if it's a man or a woman," Kyreol said, watching the young. "Or both."

"That, too."

"Well," Miko said, turning back to her work, "don't let me stop you. Ask them."

It took one image of Wayfarer on the screen, one drawing by Kyreol in the dust of Thanos, and half a dozen points before the aliens stopped gazing at her with their immobile faces and began conversing among themeslves.

"Thanos," they said in their ghostly voices. "Thanos. Kyreol. Ship."

"But how," Kyreol asked bewilderedly, "do they say yes?"

They said yes quite simply, patting the image of Wayfarer and then their heads.

Joss laughed, delighted, and was startled again by their echoes of his laughter.

Kyreol watched them, wondering at the questions that must be going through their heads: What were these strange beings, wearing replaceable skin instead of fur, who changed their entire faces instead of their eye color, who leaked water when they were distressed and bared rows of a hard white substance in their faces at unexpected moments? Miko tossed her hands in the air and swung away from the computer, grinning. What would that mean? The gesture and the teeth. But by now, she reasoned, they must be recognizing smiles.

The panel spoke, and Miko spun back to it.

"Wayfarer." The voice crackled, sounding very far away. "This is the Dome. We have received your message. We are immensely relieved. Please keep hourly contact with us on your voyage home. We have notified families of survivors and of the dead. Preparations will be made to receive them. The message to Nara was relayed to North Outstation Five; she will be in contact with the station from within the Riverworld. Repeat: We are delighted. Keep channels open and journey safely. End. Dome."

15

KYREOL EASED the little pickup craft to earth at
Outstation Five and got out. She stood alone, letting
the wind cool the sweat on her face. After the blank-
ness of Niade's moon, the green trees and the scarlet
birds seemed a fortune of color. Yellow wildflowers
brushed the edge of the landing strip; the sky was a
deep autumn blue. She frowned at her surroundings,
uneasy and lonely at the thought of making the long
hike to the Riverworld by herslf. Nara was still there,
and Regny, and Terje. None of them had been in the
Dome when she returned. They were caught up in
some disturbing event, which must be more important
than her brush with death and her strange experi-
ences. They had all left her.

The people at the Dome—Joss Tappan especially—
had begged her not to go. *You need rest*, he had said,
and, *Kyreol, you're being unreasonable*. And finally:
At least take someone with you.

I want Terje, she had said inflexibly. *I want to see*

my mother. I want to understand my dreams, and I can't wait until anyone has time to come with me. So she had flown, the day after she returned to the Dome, yearning for Terje, for Nara, for those whom she needed most to welcome her home. *If they won't come to me, I'll go to them,* she told Joss. *I need them.*

She took a backpack out of the craft and began to walk.

She reached the Riverworld at sunset. The smell of the River, the soft bird calls, the mist of gently fading light made her feel strange: a child again, the Kyreol who fished and picked berries and had never heard of the Dome. Most of the people were in their houses cooking supper. A boat glided past her; a couple of fishermen waved to her. Their faces were vaguely familiar, and they looked pleased yet unsurprised by her, as if people from the past, from the Dome, held no mystery, but were simply another part of the constantly shifting patterns of the World.

She swallowed, shaken and astonished by their acceptance. Tears pricked her eyes suddenly. She wanted to sit down and cry; and she realized then how terrified she still was, of the crash, the appallingly lonely moon, the alien, of the life she had chosen, where death could come at any moment, out of nowhere, and leave her bones strewn on a barren moon whose name she had never learned.

But here was her own planet underfoot, recognizing her, finally beginning to welcome her. She walked upriver to Icrane's house, not knowing where else to go. Her hands trembling; her whole body felt weak.

She had waited, it seemed, this long, for this secure place, before she could permit herself to be completely afraid.

The door of the Healer's house was closed. She stood helplessly in front of it, afraid to open it, wondering if it would only open to emptiness. It opened abruptly.

Nara was holding her. Kyreol couldn't speak. She stood shaking, gripping Nara tightly, gazing into the little house, her eyes dry, stunned with memories.

"Kyreol," Nara whispered. "Kyreol."

"You're always leaving me at the wrong time," she said.

"I'm sorry, I'm sorry . . ."

"Well," Kyreol said. Her voice sounded high, distant, unfamiliar. "What are you doing here, anyway?"

"Come inside."

"Are you ever coming back to the Dome?"

"Kyreol, please come inside." Another face appeared over Nara's shoulder: a hunter. The Hunter.

"Regny," Kyreol whispered, and began to cry a little then, because the whole world was turning upside down. He looked amazed, more disturbed by her then, than by anything else she had ever done.

"I know the Healer is dead," she said. "But I don't know why Terje painted his face like that. Our ship crashed on one of Niade's moons. I wasn't hurt, but two people died. Joss Tappan didn't. Where is Terje?"

Nara's grip had slackened. "How do you know? Kyreol, how do you know these things?"

"They kept sending me dreams. Both of them. I was there, alone on that moon but for an alien who couldn't talk to me, but I kept seeing things: Someone was dying; Terje was holding the River; I didn't know which one of them had died, and I didn't know where Joss was, or even where I was. And you weren't there when I finally got back. Yesterday. So I flew here."

Regny breathed something. "Kyreol," he began, but his voice had vanished.

"Where is Terje?"

"He's upriver, at the Face, I think," Nara said. For some reason, the simple answer, or Terje's nearness, was soothing. Kyreol was silent a moment. Nara still held her tightly, stroking the tears and dust on her face. Finally, she felt her trembling begin to ease. Perhaps she could take a step, perhaps she could take another. The Face sounded like a good place to be then, and she knew all the places Terje might be. And even if there was one more secret place, she would find it.

She felt Nara take a deep breath, loose it. "I promised we would stay until he returned," she explained. "I didn't expect you to return so soon. Kyreol, I didn't know which of you needed me most."

Me, Kyreol thought. But, remembering Icrane's death, Terje's masked face, she was suddenly unsure herself.

"Well," she said finally. "I came here to find you."

That, for some reason, made Nara cry.

Regny made them both some tea. The house, still full of the Healer's possessions, seemed stripped bare without Icrane. All Kyreol's childhood was gone from it, she realized slowly; it had died with Icrane. There was a fish stew bubbling on the firebed, nut-bread and late berries in leaves. Regny put a great bowl of food in her hands. She ate one bite, then just held it, warming her icy hands, while he and Nara tried to tell her what happened.

"Terje said what?" she kept saying. "He did what?" Their words made sense but no sense. She put the bowl down finally, knowing that her brain would never make sense of anything until Terje told her.

"Why did he leave?"

"It's part of the ritual," Nara said. "The new Healer must go to the Face. Where, only Terje knows. I'm worried about him. He's been gone so long."

They were explaining, but they weren't telling her what she most needed to know. She needed to see his face, look into his eyes, and ask him.

Terje. Are you leaving me?

She stirred restlessly. Then she stood up, knowing what she had to do. "I'm going to find him."

They looked at her silently, worried, pleading. But they had no other answers for her.

Regny only said, "Finish your stew first."

She ate it quickly, in silence. Nara watched her without moving, the other woman of the Dome who had found her way back to the Riverworld. To bury her husband. Kyreol swallowed fish around a lump in her throat. She looked at her mother finally.

"I'm sorry," she whispered. There was nothing more to be said. Nara smiled, her habitually grave face showing many things in the firelight: sadness, memories, acceptance, wonder, even an odd contentment that had never been there before.

"He proved me wrong," she said. "In spite of everything I worked for, Icrane brought the Dome to the Riverworld."

Kyreol rose. She bent, kissed Nara's cheek quickly.

Regny said, "Be careful. You've only got a couple more hours of dusk."

"I can make it. My feet know all the trails. Will you be here?" she demanded, and Nara closed her eyes.

"Kyreol. This time, I promise."

AS QUICKLY as she walked, the sky had turned a deep, soft sapphire by the time she reached the trail up the Falls. A solitary planet burned above the Face: Xtal, the world she had never reached. Perhaps, next time, she would make it. The Falls roared past her; spray clung to her hair, her clothes. She remembered the last time she had taken that path and was amazed that she had ever been so young. Kyreol, face painted for her betrothal, child of the Riverworld. Even then, the Hunter had come into her life, disturbing, with his soundless step, the patterns of her life.

The colors of the twilight, the endless, mighty downpouring of the River, the worn trail itself up damp earth and wet stone were her heritage. She moved among them by right, and with love, knowing that however tiny the Riverworld was, the planet itself was tiny, a bright stone in the river of the night, and all things on it, in the eons of the planet's existence, had become connected. Terje had known that, somehow. Terje had always known.

The path curved abruptly behind the Falls. She slipped onto the ledge, stood catching her breath. It was dark there between the River and the Face. She would have to feel her way. But she wasn't afraid. Her body still remembered the shape of the Riverworld, all the times, in day or darkness, she had found its hidden places.

She walked slowly past the ritual caves. She knew them by the sudden yawn in solid stone of a deeper black, a rush of chilled air. These places, except for the betrothal cave, she had never entered. She felt no hesitation now; if Terje were in one—even in the most sacred of them—she would enter. She needed him. The River was the World, and the World would forgive her.

But he wasn't in any of them. Unless he lay dreaming on cold stone in total darkness. And that made no sense: where there was ritual, there was fire.

Maybe he was in trouble. She stopped, halfway across the Falls, perplexed. *Terje, where are you?* Then she saw, on the other side of the Falls, a misty blur of light.

There was a jagged crevice in the far wall. She stepped inside.

He had painted his face again. There were small paint pots on the floor of the cave. Also an oil lamp, a mat, a fur blanket. There were birds all over his face. He, too, had flown away somewhere. He sat on the mat, gazing at the flame, frowning slightly, as someone might frown, concentrating, during a dream.

She whispered, "Terje."

He blinked, raised his head slowly; she couldn't see,

beyond the colorful patterns of birds, the expression on his face. All around her, the walls were painted, rich with centuries of Healers' first visions.

He got to his feet, stumbling a little. "Kyreol?" *Are you a dream, too?* Then he reached her, reached out for her; she felt the chill of his skin and the warmth of his love. "Kyreol!"

She closed her eyes, holding him so tightly their breaths stopped. "Terje." She blinked back tears. He kissed her, again and again, until she laughed. But her voice came in a wail. "Terje, what are you doing here?"

"You came. You came here."

"Well, I had to. Terje, look at your face. It's full of birds."

He touched it, remembering. "I was flying . . . dreaming. The birds were teaching me . . ."

She shook her head wordlessly, suddenly exasperated by the twists and turns of the River. "Oh, Terje. I leave you for ten days and you turn yourself into a Healer."

"I'm sorry."

"Now what are we going to do?"

He kissed her again. He didn't seem worried by the problem. He held her face between his hands, then explored her body lightly, anxiously. "Were you hurt in the crash?"

She shook her head. "I'm fine." She hid her eyes against his shoulder. "I was so frightened. I was alone with the dead on an empty moon . . ."

He stroked her hair, swallowing. "Icrane dreamed of you."

"He sent me dreams. You both did. They got all mixed up—I didn't know which of you had died. For a while. Then I knew. Terje, are you—are you ever coming back to the Dome?"

He looked at her; the peace in his eyes was the peace of the Riverworld. "What do you think?" he asked. "Look at me."

"Your face—"

"My face is next to your face. My arms are around you. I'm so hungry I can hardly stand up, but I can't let go of you."

"But, Terje—"

"Icrane opened a door between the Dome and the Riverworld. You came through it. So can I. It leads to the same place."

"You can't just wander back and forth between two worlds—"

"Why not? I've been doing it ever since I came to the Dome. Every ritual-time, I made my way back . . . Kyreol . . ." He put his cheek against hers, his arms shifting to draw her closer. "I'd never leave you," he whispered. "Not even for this. I told Icrane that."

"What did he say?"

"He smiled."

She was silent, trying to envision their unpredictable future. "But Terje, what about little things? People having bad dreams, children getting bitten by snakes, pregnant women needing teas. All that is part of being a Healer."

"What about you flying off to Xtal. You talking to aliens? You visiting dream caves on other planets?

At least, when you need me, you'll know where to find me."

"I'll need you," she whispered. He was silent; the birds on his face seemed to move in the flickering light.

"Kyreol, I had no choice. The Riverworld made the choice."

"I can see that. But—"

"I needed you. And you came. It was that simple."

Her voice rose. "It was not simple! I had to come to you across space, and then fly myself across two worlds, from the future into the past—"

"You came," he said again. She gazed at him, speechless, and wondered which of them was right. Was the complexity of the world what kept her, from moment to moment, always on the edge of wonder? Or was the wonder that it was simple, that she could turn across space and time, and there would be Terje? Terje kissed her open mouth, left her without an argument.

His hold loosened finally; he rubbed at the birds, blinking dizzily. "I'd better get back down the Face while I still have the strength. But first I have to—" He looked around vaguely for the paints. Kyreol sat down on the stones.

"May I watch? Or is it secret?"

"I want you to watch."

She glanced around at all the paintings on the walls: animals, dream-faces, designs, all crowded together, the Healers' first comments as they woke from their long journey into knowledge. Terje found a clear space, moved the lamp so he could see. Kyreol composed herself quietly. The dreaming was private, a message from Terje to himself. She wouldn't ask; she would wait patiently, respectfully, for the image to form under his fingers . . . She wouldn't ask . . .

"Terje. What are you going to paint?"

He smiled. "You."

Sword And Sorcery At Its Finest!

MICHAEL MOORCOCK

Fantasy from Ace
fanciful and fantastic!